PENGUIN BOOKS

DEATH IN SUMMER

'A veteran Trevor novel, with its lucid, spare prose, its air of menace and its social acuity. There is extraordinary sympathy here for people of such very different worlds, which clash with vertiginous results'
Catherine Pepinster, *Independent on Sunday*

'"Compassionate" is the word most frequently used to describe William Trevor's attitude to the world … compassion is indeed an ingredient here, along with clear-sightedness and an elegance of diction that is approaching ever more closely to the elegiac' Patricia Craig, *Independent*

'He is unique, consistently making the ordinary and familiar new and shocking' Eileen Battersby, *Irish Times*

'For forty years, William Trevor has created, unequalled, a world of the commonplace, and has rendered it extraordinary. It is peopled with goodness and evil, with secret selves discreetly awash with foolish fear, with discontent, with hope, with irreducible, ineluctable longing. Each time it comes to us newly minted yet wholly familiar. He is the master of the singular human life' Tom Adair, *Scotland on Sunday*

'His narrative voice is as icy as any crime writer's, yet there is an unmistakeable humanity in the small details it chooses to illuminate'
Patrick Gale, *Daily Telegraph*

William Trevor was born in 1928 at Mitchelstown, County Cork, and he spent his childhood in provincial Ireland. He attended a number of Irish schools and later Trinity College, Dublin. He is a member of the Irish Academy of Letters. He has written many novels, including *The Old Boys* (1964), winner of the Hawthornden Prize; *The Children of Dynmouth* (1976) and *Fools of Fortune* (1983), both winners of the Whitbread Fiction Award; *The Silence in the Garden* (1988), winner of the Yorkshire Post Book of the Year Award; *Two Lives* (1991), which was shortlisted for the Sunday Express Book of the Year Award and includes the Booker shortlisted novella *Reading Turgenev*; *Felicia's Journey* (1994), which won both the Whitbread Book of the Year and the Sunday Express Book of the Year awards; and *Death in Summer* (1998). A celebrated short-story writer, his most recent collection is *After Rain* (1996). He is also the editor of *The Oxford Book of Irish Short Stories* (1989). He has written plays for the stage and for radio and television; several of his television plays have been based on his short stories. Most of his books are published in Penguin.

In 1976 William Trevor received the Allied Irish Banks' Prize, and in 1977 was awarded an honorary CBE in recognition of his valuable services to literature. In 1992 he received the Sunday Times Award for Literary Excellence and in 1999 he was awarded the prestigious David Cohen British Literature Prize in recognition of a lifetime's literary achievement. Many critics and writers have praised his work: he is to Hilary Mantel he 'one of the contemporary writers I most admire' and to Carol Shields 'a worthy chronicler of our times'. In the *Spectator* Anita Brookner wrote 'These novels will endure. And in every beautiful sentence there is not a word out of place,' and John Banville believes William Trevor's to be 'among the most subtle and sophisticated fiction being written today'.

Death in Summer

WILLIAM TREVOR

PENGUIN BOOKS

PENGUIN BOOKS

Published by the Penguin Group
Penguin Books Ltd, 27 Wrights Lane, London w8 5tz, England
Penguin Putnam Inc., 375 Hudson Street, New York, New York 10014, USA
Penguin Books Australia Ltd, Ringwood, Victoria, Australia
Penguin Books Canada Ltd, 10 Alcorn Avenue, Toronto, Ontario, Canada m4v 3b2
Penguin Books (NZ) Ltd, Private Bag 102902, NSMC, Auckland, New Zealand

Penguin Books Ltd, Registered Offices: Harmondsworth, Middlesex, England

First published by Viking 1998
Published in Penguin Books 1999
1 3 5 7 9 10 8 6 4 2

Set in 12.5 on 16.25 pt Monotype Bembo
Phototypeset by Intype London Ltd
Printed in England by Clays Ltd, St Ives plc

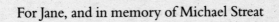

For Jane, and in memory of Michael Streat

After the funeral the hiatus that tragedy brought takes a different form. The suddenness of the death has gone, irrelevant now. Thaddeus has stood and knelt in the church of St Nicholas, has heard his wife called good, the word he himself gave to a clergyman he has known all his life. People were present in the church who were strangers to him, who afterwards, in the house, introduced themselves as a few of Letitia's friends from the time before he knew her. 'And where is Letitia now?' an undertaker a week ago inquired, confusing Thaddeus, who for a moment wondered if the man knew why he had been summoned. 'It's Letitia who has died,' he said, and answered, when the man explained, that Letitia was in the mortuary, where she'd been taken.

All that is over now, and yet is coldly there in the first moment of waking every day: the coffin, the flowers laid out, the bright white surplice of the clergyman, dust to dust, and that seeming an insensitive expression at the time. There is Letitia's mother in the graveyard, and some cousin, and a chubby woman whose bed was next but one to Letitia's in a school dormitory more than twenty years ago. And there are all the others: local people, and colleagues from the music library, the postman who retired two years ago and was particularly fond of Letitia, the twins who come to clean the windows. There are the tears on Zenobia's plump cheeks, and Maidment gaunt and appalled. The day the heatwave began it was, that funeral afternoon, the empty blue of the sky touched upon in the clergyman's brief eulogy. For as long as he lives, Thaddeus Davenant believes those funeral images will be there in the first moment of his waking.

He is a spare, handsome man in his mid-forties, with pale brown eyes beneath hair that almost matches them. Inheritor of a property set in the flatlands of Essex, he has been solitary even in marriage, this the legacy of an unusual childhood, compounded by his choosing to eke out a livelihood selling the produce of his garden rather than seeking to discover a vocation or otherwise claiming a profession.

Quincunx House, once more remote than it is now, was built by a tallow merchant, John Percival Davenant, in 1896, its name deriving from the five wild cherry trees he ordered to be planted, one at each corner of his high-walled garden, one at its centre. Many years later this garden became Thaddeus's greatest pleasure. In it, he still saves his own seeds, and cultivates hellebores people would come to see if they knew about them. He has replaced decaying heathers with growth from their own new shoots. He has teased a vine back to life in his conservatory. He has been successful with blue poppies and the most difficult penstemons.

Among the memories that linger after the funeral there is Letitia learning the secrets of the garden – how to prune the wistaria, when to trim the yew, cosseting the ceanothus when frost threatened. There is Letitia resting beneath the catalpa tree, pregnant with the child she has left behind. Six years ago Thaddeus brought her here, Letitia Iveson, a person of almost wayward generosity, although she never saw herself in such a light: plainness was what Letitia had seen and sighed over since adolescence and before. Thaddeus did not so harshly judge, finding in her features a tranquillity that challenged beauty with a distinction of its own: a Piero della Francesca face, he insisted with only a little exaggeration.

Before becoming a wife Letitia had lived with her mother in the spacious flat near Regent's Park where she had passed her childhood, the relationship between the two bonded to some degree by the perpetual confinement of Mr Iveson in medical care. At his decree, while he still retained his senses, the Iveson family means had been divided into three: equal shares for the two women and for his nursing home. Twice a year, wife and daughter took a train to Bath, where this home – St Bee's – spread through two houses in a crescent. Five times a week Letitia walked to the music library in Marylebone, her services at the disposal of musicologists and biographers, the reading-room her particular province. An ageing virgin, she considered herself then, and did not think much about marriage, since there had never been a reason to until Thaddeus came into her life.

In fact, though certainly ageing, Letitia became a younger wife. Her wealth restored the derelict state of Quincunx House, allowed the employment of a couple as cook and houseman, and dispensed with the necessity for Thaddeus to sell the garden's fruit and vegetables. With difficulty, and after several disappointments, a daughter, Georgina, was born.

It had been Letitia's wish, not Thaddeus's, that there should be a child but, while wondering at the time what it was going to be like to have a baby about the place, he did not demur, and soon after Georgina's birth was surprised to find his feelings quite startlingly transformed. Marriage had changed everything in Letitia's life. The birth of Georgina changed, in part, Thaddeus. Wizened and blotched, as tiny as a doll, she was Letitia's object: Thaddeus imagined that would always be so and did not expect otherwise. But within a fortnight he found himself claiming his daughter, possessed by an affection he had been unable to feel for anyone since his own infancy.

All that is memory, too: images and moments that join the details of the funeral occasion, the lowered tones of the clergyman, a silence asked for. But most of all – remembered also by the household's couple – is the last afternoon of Letitia's life. Because of her disposition and Thaddeus's practice in his marriage of saying too little rather than too much – her natural inclination to amity, his to mild prevarication – there was not often a disagreement between the two. But a drizzling Thursday in June had been affected since early morning by unusual inquietude: in passing a letter across the breakfast table, Thaddeus had blundered. Better, he later realized, to have slipped it into a pocket, as occasionally he did with awkward correspondence at breakfast-time. That morning he was careless, allowing himself to sigh over Mrs Ferry's missive, and Letitia had smiled in sympathy and asked him what it was. He should have shaken his head and been evasive. Instead, he thought he might as well confess this continuing nuisance. 'Haven't I mentioned Mrs Ferry before?' he asked, knowing he hadn't but feeling that such an introduction was necessary. Letitia's denial allowed him a description, which he lightly gave while the letter's contents were read. But he knew when the single sheet of violet-coloured writing-paper was handed back across the table that he'd been foolish.

He knew it even more certainly when the matter was raised again in the afternoon. At breakfast, about to crumple the letter into a ball, muddling it with the junk mail that had come, he changed his mind. He returned Mrs Ferry's communication to its envelope and placed it beside him on the tablecloth, the gesture implying that he intended to sit down and compose a reply, and to send what Mrs Ferry was after, which was a cheque for fifty pounds.

'You've done it?' Letitia pressed in the afternoon.

'This evening. I promise.'

The french windows of the drawing-room were misted with tiny droplets that did not merge to run down the glass: Thaddeus remembers that afterwards. He remembers the agitation in Letitia's voice, and a pale tinge coming into the flesh of her round face – not brought about by jealousy of Mrs Ferry, for that would be ridiculous, but by her concern for a woman she did not know, who clearly had been on her mind all day, a woman he himself hadn't laid eyes on for all of seventeen years.

'Please, Thaddeus. She's far from well.'

'I doubt it's true, you know, much of what she says about not being well.'

'Why shouldn't it be true? Poor creature, why shouldn't she be alone and ill?'

In the dining-room, registering the exchanges through the door that is common to both rooms, Maidment learnt that Mrs Ferry's plea for assistance was also a reminder that she had repeatedly written before and not once received an

5

answer. The poor woman was wretched with stomach ulcers and related suffering, came a further rebuke through the door panels. She called herself a charity case: afterwards Maidment particularly remembers that being said.

'But, Letty, she would call herself anything to get money.'

'And you have given her none? In all the years she mentions?'

'I could not give Mrs Ferry your money, which is what it would amount to. I could not do that, and I had none to spare before.'

'Please give her something now.'

'If you would like me to I shall.'

'Please.'

In the dining-room Maidment nodded to himself. His perusal of Mrs Ferry's previous letters had not been confessed to his wife, whose disapproval could be biting when she put it into words. Eavesdropping Zenobia accepted, as conversation unavoidably overheard; the investigation of private correspondence, and poking about in drawers, she preferred to believe did not occur. So Maidment had kept to himself what he had long ago pieced together: that the woman who wrote the begging letters was guilty of the sin of profitable nostalgia; of resurrecting one or two good moments so that, in the circumstances as they were now, the past might be honoured with a cheque. The woman's handwriting sprawled wildly, decorated with exclamation marks and underlining, Maidment recalled, listening again to the voices in the drawing-room.

'Don't laugh at her, Thaddeus.'

Although the keyhole of the connecting door contained no key, Maidment did not stoop to a more intimate witnessing of the scene. He did not see Thaddeus – in pale corduroy trousers, tweed jacket and tie – standing in front of the empty fire-place, nor observe the holding back of Letitia's tears. The deep blue of her dress reflecting the dots of sapphire in her earrings, her fair hair plaited in a coil, she stood also, pressed into the corner by the door, as though her sympathy for Mrs Ferry consigned her there. Her dog – a retriever she had found as a puppy, drowning in a ditch – was stretched out between the two sets of french windows, half an eye on the misty garden outside.

'I'll do whatever you say, Letty. This is too little a thing to disagree about.'

Maidment carried that plea to the kitchen. 'If there's going to be quarrelling between them,' he gloomily predicted, 'it'll be the end of us.'

In retrospect, a few hours later, there is a harshness in the statement that passed unnoticed at the time. Phlegmatic and an optimist, Zenobia simply retorted that if he was talking about separation or divorce he was being altogether too pessimistic. Married couples disagreed, as they had observed both in a personal way and in their experience of other households. The infant born four and a half months ago in this one will become a child with characteristics and a nature of her own, an influence for stability and for good should such an influence be needed, which Zenobia doubted. Colouring her argument, she touched upon the occasion of the birth: cherry brandy poured in the kitchen at a quarter past eleven at night, she herself clapping her hands, then clasping them to give thanks, Mrs Iveson in the house as the prospective grandmother, the midwife brisk and self-important, the January night damply mild. After the gloom of miscarrying in the past it had been the happiest of events and most certainly boded well.

'Added to which they do not row at all, those two.'

When first they came to the house, before Maidment made his way through past and present correspondence, and listened in on the kitchen telephone when Zenobia's back was turned, the Maidments' impression was that Thaddeus Davenant's wife had done well for herself. They had not known the house gone to rack and ruin, and did not then realize the circumstances of its rescue. Now they knew everything.

'I'm only saying,' Maidment defended himself. 'I'm only telling what's said.'

'They're suited. We both know that.'

Favouring black in clothes worn tightly, accentuating plumpness, Zenobia has soft hazel eyes in a soft face, her cheeks streaked like two good apples, her hair flecked with the grey her forty-nine years demand. In contrast, her husband is a hawk-faced man, dark-jowled and lankly made, his servant's wear – black also – completing the priestly look he cultivates. Second to his servant's curiosity, Maidment's interest is the turf.

'Their natures complement one another,' Zenobia's insistence firmly went on. 'That is important.'

Leaving the kitchen with cloths and a tin of Mansion polish, Maidment did not pause to comment on that. Strengths and weaknesses were distributed to the marriage's advantage, Zenobia's view was, and neither party trespassed on ground that was already claimed: alone again in her particular domain she reflected on that, and saw the future bright.

'Please go to her,' Maidment heard, his cloths on the dining-room table, the lid taken from the polish tin. A hole-in-corner thing, he concluded, a long-ago affair his employer could hardly be blamed for not wishing to pick over.

'*Go* to her? She doesn't actually ask—'

'Darling, she asks for reassurance and a little money. A dying woman who is alone, Thaddeus.'

'She doesn't actually say she's dying.'

Heard by Maidment but not seen, the dog, called Rosie, yawned, then pushed herself on to her feet, slipping about on the polished boards with a scrabble of paws. She settled herself again and, while the two familiar voices continued, slept.

Thaddeus was patient and conciliatory. Quarrels were pointless; they did no good; nothing was ever gained. He had been careless, he was to blame. But even so this need not become more tiresome than it was already, and visiting Mrs Ferry would certainly be as tiresome as anything he could imagine.

'I'll write, Letty. It's all she wants. It was nineteen seventy-nine when I knew her. It would be awfully difficult, meeting again.'

Dot she'd been in 1979, not Mrs Ferry, as somehow in Thaddeus's thoughts she had since become. Receptionist at the Beech Trees Hotel – two AA stars – she had married Ferry, who was its manager, sharing his duties when they returned from honeymooning. A little later she'd been unfaithful to him in Room Twenty. Airless and poky, with windows opening on to the hotel's well, Room Twenty had been suitable for surreptitious afternoon love, being tucked away and quiet. 'Two of a kind, dear,' the husky voice came back to Thaddeus, the fleshy limbs, hair dyed a shade of henna. 'Bad hats, bad news,' Mrs Ferry liked to whisper in Room Twenty, an older woman who'd been around, who had renamed the cocktail bar the Pink Lady and the dining-room The Chandeliers. She folded underclothes on to the one chair the room supplied and afterwards, putting them on again, often spoke about her husband, her voice gone slack, touched with disdain. 'Tried going without it, dear, but it doesn't work.' His sandy moustache was what he tried to go without; he had a gammy leg as well. A likeable enough man in Thaddeus's memory, who would presumably have left her years ago.

'Please, Thaddeus.'

'If you really want me to, of course I'll go to see her.'

He smiled although he did not feel like smiling. It wasn't necessary to visit the woman and he did not intend to. He wondered if the nature of the relationship had crossed Letitia's mind, if even for a passing moment it had occurred to her that the woman she wished to see assisted had been his associate in passionate intimacy, that they had deceived a decent man, carelessly gratifying desire. Even after six years of marriage he didn't know his wife well enough. She could have suspected everything or nothing: her tone gave no clue when next she spoke, only a freshness in it marking the end of the contretemps.

'This summer will be an idyll,' she said, and he knew she meant because it was Georgina's first. A quality in Letitia often anticipated happiness, and for a moment Thaddeus regretted his own shortcomings in this respect.

'I have the pullet chicks to collect this afternoon.' She

smiled and crossed the room to kiss him. 'Thanks for doing the box.'

That morning he had attached a wooden box to the carrier of her bicycle, large enough to contain the six chicks she had arranged to fetch. Since she did not drive, Letitia cycled about the lanes – to collect honey from a bee-keeper she had got to know, or tomatoes because Thaddeus didn't grow them any more, or to call in to see old Mrs Parch or Abbie Mates. Even when it was cold, or raining quite hard, she preferred cycling to walking or being driven. She had made the lanes her own, local people approvingly remarked to Thaddeus, and he agreed that his wife knew the lanes well by now.

'I'll settle Georgina in the garden before I go. The sun is trying to come out at last.'

Thaddeus opened the french windows, Rosie lunged to her feet. Why Letitia should wish to keep chickens would once have been bewildering, as would her concern for a woman she had never laid eyes on. She didn't know about chickens. She won't know whether the half-dozen shown to her are good of their kind or not. Nor will she know if the man selling them is telling the truth about their being disease-free or about whatever other hazards there may be. She will believe the man, every single word he utters, and somehow her purchases will survive disease and lay the eggs expected of them: when Letitia trusted to luck she was more often than not rewarded. This irrational trust, and Letitia's goodness, the practical steeliness of her resolve, were entangled in a nature that was disarmingly humble. It was his considerable loss, Thaddeus was every day aware, that he did not love his wife.

'Yes, it's going to be sunny,' he agreed.

That morning, too, he had constructed a coop, eight posts driven into an out-of-the-way patch of ground, chicken-wire stapled into place, a crude door, mostly of chicken-wire also. The pullets will spend only their nights in it, safe from the jaws of foxes. By day, they'll scratch about among the silver birches.

'I don't think I should be long,' Letitia predicted. 'An hour maybe.'

'I'll cut the grass.'

'You'll keep an eye on Georgina?'

'Yes, of course.'

In the dining-room Maidment gathered up his cloths and polish tin. In the kitchen Zenobia beat up eggs for a sponge cake, saying to herself that one of these Sundays they must drive over to see the Scarrow Man, a wonder cut from the turf of Scarrow Hill. Georgina was wheeled into the garden, and settled beneath the big catalpa tree in case the sun became bright.

Later, Maidment watched his employer throwing an old tennis ball for his wife's dog, then starting up the lawn-mower, although in Maidment's opinion the grass was still too wet to cut. *Why don't you make a sign?* a previous communication from Mrs Ferry had chided, the violet writing-paper stained in a corner with a splash of some-thing yellow, which he had unproductively sniffed. *I am a nuisance perhaps. Or are you gone away? 'Has the old house become too much for him?' I say to myself. 'Has he ages ago gone from it and do my letters lie dusty in the hall, picked up by no one? Yet how attached he was to that house!' I say again. 'It would fall down around him yet he would not leave!' How much a single line would mean! That and any little you can spare a needy friend.*

Maidment's reconstruction of the friendship had established that Mrs Ferry was aware his employer was married now. She was not in the business of making trouble, she had assured, each word of that underlined twice. But neither that nor her belief that the house had been abandoned rang true. What did was what wasn't written: that she had come to know there was money where once there hadn't been. There was a taste of blackmail here, in Maidment's view.

In the kitchen Zenobia's sponge cake cooled on a wire tray, and when Georgina was in the house again and Maidment was laying the dining-room table Thaddeus pushed the lawnmower over the cobbles of the yard, its engine still running, the grass of the two lawns now cropped close. He turned the ignition off and, watched by Rosie, her shaggy head interestedly on one side, he hosed away the debris of clippings from the blades. Letitia was taking longer than she'd said and he imagined her asking questions at whatever farm it was she had gone to, and listening to the answers in her careful way.

The clock in the hall was striking six when the two policemen came.

2

There is Georgina to consider now: Letitia's mother says that first, and Thaddeus wonders if somewhere beneath that comment there is Mrs Iveson's wish to bring up her grand-child herself. There is no reason why the thought should not be there, why Mrs Iveson should not have envisaged Georgina in the flat near Regent's Park, why grandmother and grandchild should not belong together, both being alone in the world. The assumption that he will not come up to scratch as a father on his own seems to Thaddeus to be a natural projection of Mrs Iveson's more general opinion of him.

But on the telephone one morning, just over a week after the funeral, nothing of that outrageous kind is mentioned. Instead, Mrs Iveson speaks of the employment of a nanny. 'I'll help you choose one,' she offers, 'if you would like me to.'

Taken aback, for he had not considered such a necessity, Thaddeus hesitates before replying. 'You feel I should take on a nanny?' he responds eventually.

'I rather think, you know, Letitia would want us to. If you advertise,' Mrs Iveson quietly continues, seeming to Thaddeus to have taken charge of the matter, 'I'd come and look the possibles over.'

'It's kind of you.'

'You'll phone me when you've had a few replies?' And

Mrs Iveson suggests where the advertisement should be placed and the form some of its wording should take. It is a woman's thing, Thaddeus tells himself, and therefore understandable that his mother-in-law should slip into this role: she is not by nature a domineering person.

'Yes, I'll be in touch,' he agrees. 'I'm very grateful.'

So, for the moment, the matter is left. 'A girl is to be taken on,' Maidment reports in the kitchen. 'Mrs Iveson to have a hand in the appointment. Which stands to reason.'

It is Zenobia who later draws attention to the little room next to the nursery, which long ago nannies must have occupied. She puts it to Thaddeus that she should run up new curtains for it, and a matching bedspread while she's at it. The windowsill and skirting-board could do with a coat of paint, and Maidment does that work on the afternoon of the Derby, a transistor radio turned low beside him.

While the advertisement is placed and replies to it awaited, the hiatus that affects the household continues. Kept private, disguised as best he can, melancholy is Thaddeus's natural state. The cruel ending of a life aggravates this shrouded disposition, while permitting its exposure now. In the bleak aftermath of what so suddenly and so terribly occurred, as often he has on less awful occasions, Thaddeus seeks consolation in his possession of the house that long ago became his, in its rooms and garden and protective walls. The place is everything to him, is presently a comfort because its household order has so often survived the fractures of arrival and departure, of domestic drama and the finality of death. At a time when all thought is shaded by sorrow and by guilt it is reassurance of a kind that the house seems greater than its passing occupants, that effortlessly it once carried the mores of one dying century into the next, has been part monument part deity to its generations, benevolent in sunshine, bequeathing gloom through the grimness of its aspect in certain weathers. Secrets are locked into its fabric, its windows seeing and yet blind. His secrets are there too, Thaddeus knows, to be left behind one day. His wife left none, for secrets were not her way.

But given to romantic speculation, Letitia sometimes wondered if their child would be taken from the house a bride: waiting for the response to his advertisement, Thaddeus remembers that. He wonders, himself, about the brides of the past, not knowing that when the cherry trees rose hardly six feet above the earth the first bride drove with her father to the country church of St Nicholas and experienced a moment of doubt on the way to the altar, where Nevil James Limewell waited to make her his wife. There were more than a hundred guests at Quincunx House that day, with extra servants hired. The photographs taken found their way long afterwards into a collector's accumulation of such material, these nameless people of the past given an incidental place in the history of photography. The fox-terriers of the household ran among the bridesmaids and the wedding guests, and were made to beg for crumbs of cake. In the bedroom that had always been hers, while changing into the clothes she had chosen for her wedding journey, the bride experienced her second moment of doubt. Yet for months, she told herself – almost a year – she had longed for the proposal and had not hesitated when it came. She was to live in Shropshire and would be happy: this latter anticipation she spoke aloud. *Sweet visage, linger with me*, a cousin who was in love with her wrote, secretly that same evening, in the room that is now the Maidments' sitting-room.

It rained in the twilight of the first wedding day, when everything was being set to rights again and spirits were deflated after the celebration. 'We took Annie Talbot in,' Augusta Davenant reminded her husband, having held back the necessity for this conversation while all the preparations were under way. 'We gave her a home. Then this.' A parlourmaid had run off in the early hours two days ago, taking her clothes and her belongings with her. She did so at the instigation of a local groom, Robert Bantwell, who later deserted her. 'How fortunate we were with the weather!' Augusta's husband responded, seeking a distraction from prolonged talk of the servant's flight. Vexation between the two developed and for a while there were recriminations. Then children knelt in dressing-gowns to recite the Lord's Prayer, a drawing-room tradition of that time.

Three generations later – in the same month that the central cherry tree was cut down when its growth began to spoil the garden – a picture was painted on the nursery floor and is still there now. The rooks that began to nest in the oaks when the house was built have had their generations too, and rooks still claim their branches, building high or low depending on their predictions for the months to come. In the present and the past chaffinches have flown into the drawing-room; once a rabbit came, through the open french windows. Bees have stung in the kitchen and the bedrooms, wasps have nested in chimneys, flies have struggled on fly-papers, spiders have experienced the destruction of their cobwebs, workmen have scrawled their names on the bare plaster of walls. There have been thirty-one births and nineteen deaths in the house, swathed infants carried for christening to the church of St Nicholas, the dead conveyed for burial by black-plumed horses, and motor-hearses later.

By the time Thaddeus was first conscious of his surroundings the days of the Davenants' enterprise and prosperity were over. Mismanagement in a single generation had initiated decline and the aftermath of war did not permit recovery. And Thaddeus witnessed in another way the effects of that same war: in his father's failure to recover from the distress of his experiences in battle. A tattered grandeur was a shadowy backdrop to the scenes of love that were the house's only drama now: his father fondly cosseted, his Polish mother, once Eva Paczkowska, adored. Servantless, the two existed only for one another, for ever comforting and consoling, his father with silences that were all devotion, his mother with Polish endearments Thaddeus didn't understand. No dog was kept, no cat. No people came to the house except, once in a while, Father Rzadiewicz to play cards. The talk was of Poland then, Thaddeus unnoticed in the room, a card game forgotten for a while. In the garden that his mother said had once been magical he played alone, among the overgrown shrubs and shattered cold-frames, pretending sometimes that the ghosts of the pets' graveyard were there: Peko and Jet and Rory, Mickey and Felix and Dash, Peggotty and Polonius. 'I didn't like my dream,' he whispered to his mother, coming downstairs in the white nightdress she had made him. Building a house of cards, using all the pack, which he could do, his father did not turn round to hear. His mother said there was nothing to be frightened of in a dream and he felt cowardly, creeping back to bed. Tadzio his mother called him, his father Thaddeus. The obscure apostle, Father Rzadiewicz said.

★

On a summer afternoon of another dying century four nannies pass between the gateless pillars of Quincunx House and walk to their interviews on a drive darkened by high laurels and hydrangeas not yet in bloom. Maidment's greeting of each is that she might like to stroll in the garden until the time of her appointment arrives: all have come on the one convenient train. Shyly they do what has been suggested, two of the girls keeping together, having made friends on the journey, the third in the drawing-room five minutes early, the fourth on her own.

'No good, I'm afraid,' Thaddeus's verdict is when the last one has been shown the nursery and now awaits her fate in the hall.

Mrs Iveson agrees, and adds after a pause: 'What I am wondering is if I myself should be made use of.'

Something about the way she says it alerts Thaddeus to a threat that has not occurred to him: that Mrs Iveson should come to Quincunx House.

'I couldn't ask you.' The panic he experiences is kept out of his response. 'No, no, I couldn't.'

'I am available.'

A grandmother would be more than a substitute for an unsatisfactory nanny. Her tone implies that; it is not said. There is a sacrifice involved, and she would make it: that's not said, either.

'Of course, it's naturally up to you, Thaddeus.'

The girl still waiting in the hall was the least satisfactory of the applicants. Her single, badly typed reference did not ring true. The questions Mrs Iveson asked weren't confidently answered; there'd been a whiff of cigarettes. A girl they rejected earlier had more to recommend her, and Thaddeus now wishes they had settled for her.

'I don't in any way wish to impose myself, Thaddeus.'

'No, no. I know that.'

His pale eyes rake her face and see there what they always see: distrust of him that has become indifference. On a warm afternoon she is dressed with summery distinction in a linen dress, two shades of grey. Her suede shoes, smartly casual, match the lighter one. She has a way with clothes.

'It's the least I can offer.'

A dead daughter's due: Thaddeus senses that behind those words. He told her of the tragedy on the telephone, warning her that the news was very bad and would be a shock. He told her before he told anyone else, she being who she was. The hall door was still open, the two policemen only a minute gone, one grim and silent, the one who'd done the talking with a black moustache. A vase of delphiniums was in the hall, where Letitia had arranged it an hour before there was the conversation about Mrs Ferry. According to the driver of the car, she'd been distracted, looking behind her at the wooden box on her carrier as if fearing it would become dislodged, concerned for its contents. Coming round the corner, the car hadn't been going fast: a farmhand seeing to a flock of ewes reported that. 'No, there's no doubt,' Thaddeus said, and stood by the phone when he put the receiver down, not knowing where to go or what to do. Then Maidment, in shirtsleeves with red sleeve-bands on them, came into the hall and Thaddeus told him next. The telephone rang and a man's voice began about the six pullets that had been collected an hour ago, something about their care, which he'd forgotten to say earlier. Afterwards, he took them back, and insisted on returning Letitia's cheque. The driver of the car was exonerated from any possible blame.

'You would give up your flat?'

'Some arrangement could be made. I don't know what.'

In the night Mrs Iveson resolved that if the girls who came weren't right she would make her offer. She lay awake for hours, wondering if all grandmothers felt as she did, if in similar circumstances they experienced, irresistibly, the urge to have some place in a grandchild's life. Letitia's compassion hadn't always been easy to tolerate, yet in the night it felt like cruelty that others had benefited from it and her baby would not. Twice – while Mrs Iveson sighed inwardly with impatience – Letitia had paid an old alcoholic's fare back to County Mayo. And there was Kevin with his unnecessary stick, and the one who said he was a cardinal and gave a name, and Miss Cartwell invited into the flat one hot Saturday morning, bringing with her a stench of such pungency that scented sprays and the windows wide open did not succeed in sweetening the air. 'But what can you expect,' Letitia had asked with irritating reason, 'since she has been sleeping in those clothes for more than fifteen years?' Miss Cartwell still daily passes by, on her way to the St Vincent de Paul place. The one who believes himself to be a cardinal began an awful wailing when he was told Letitia was no longer alive, and later asked for a photograph.

The urge that made her give to the dispossessed would have nourished Letitia's motherhood. Steadfast in her loyalty to her husband, she would have brought her child up to respect a father simply because that was what he was. *Bereavement drags the truth out*, Mrs Iveson wrote ten days ago to a longtime friend in Sussex. *Letitia's innocence seems just a little remarkable now, and I wonder if the good are always innocent.*

'We could advertise again,' Thaddeus suggests. 'Sooner or later a perfectly suitable girl could easily walk in.'

'I rather doubt it.'

Across the room – he standing by the open french windows, she by the fire-place – Mrs Iveson's glance fails to match the composure of her tone. It is the glance of a mother who for a long time will not cease to mourn; it is at odds with the summer coolness of her clothes, the necklace of pearls and unobtrusive earrings. Businesslike, her statements pack away emotion, leaving it only in her eyes. She has never thought to leave her flat, but once upon a time she thought Letitia would never leave it either. And Letitia did so permanently; she does not intend that.

Yet even after she made her resolution in the night Mrs Iveson hesitated all over again. No one can predict what living at close quarters with a man who has married your daughter for her money will be like. There's an elusiveness about Thaddeus that defies prediction, that did so when first he came into their lives, a stranger on a train on a Saturday afternoon, when they were returning from another visit to Bath. He talked more easily on that occasion than she has ever known since, saying he had been to see an elderly relative whom he hardly knew, who was unwell, and in what seemed an artless way confessing he had expectations from that direction. They listened to revelations about this ailing relative on his father's side, and about the house he had years ago inherited and how he made his living. They told him, when he asked, about themselves.

The landscape still changes for Mrs Iveson on that journey, the backs of houses coming when there is a town, then bright green hills again. It was April then, their first leaves decorating ash and beech. He always went on journeys of more than a certain length by train, the man who talked to them divulged, not trusting an aged car; not that, in fact, he travelled much. His voice was educated, pleasant to listen to; the encounter passed the time. But though he appeared to be quite open, she knew he wasn't. Long afterwards, when the friendship with Letitia had begun, she did not ever quite say that he was shoddy goods. Letitia said it for her, actually using the expression that had been withheld. 'You think so, don't you?' And unconvincingly Mrs Iveson denied it.

'Having seen these girls today, I can assure you I would be happier with this.' She would be seventy when she returned to her flat, Georgina no longer in need of her care. But it should not be beyond her to pick up whatever threads remained. 'You understand, Thaddeus?'

'Yes, I do.'

Thaddeus looks out, over lawns and flower-beds, at the summer-house in the distance, at the little orchard of plum trees behind it, the birch trees beyond. He might still say no. He might insist, not just suggest, that they should try with another advertisement. Or he might somehow wriggle out of what appears to have already come about. He would have, with Letitia; he would have managed something. But it is his mother-in-law who speaks next.

'Well, we cannot keep this last one waiting. In fairness, we must send her on her way.'

While speaking, she moves towards the door, taking from beneath a candlestick on the mantelpiece the last of the ten-pound notes Thaddeus earlier placed there to ensure that the girls who came weren't out of pocket after their journey. Letitia's money, Mrs Iveson can't help thinking, and wants to ask, as often she has wanted to in the weeks that have passed, 'Why did you let her cycle about the lanes?' But in fairness such a question cannot be put and she does not do so.

'Say I'm sorry,' Thaddeus requests, watching her leave the room, her back held so straight that she might only yesterday have had her last deportment lesson. His own mother did not hold herself so well when she aged. Wrapped in her damson-coloured dressing-gown, shabby at the edges, she was restless sometimes in this room, happier when she walked about the garden with the husband she lived her life for. In winter they sat and watched the rain or played chess by the fire, their two bent heads reflected in the looking-glass that stretches the length of the mantelpiece. Reflected still are the spines of books on old teak shelves, *The Essays of Elia and Eliana Lamb* embossed and tooled, F. L. Hall's *History of the Indian Empire*, the Reverend W. R. Trace's *Portrait of a Clergyman, being Anecdotes and Reminiscences*, Daudier's *Fly Fishing, Great Scenes from the Courts, A Century of Horror Tales*. All of Charlotte, Anne and Emily Brontë is there, all of George Eliot and the Waverley novels, Sir Percy Keane's *Diary of an Edwardian Hell-Raiser*, all of Thackeray and Dickens. The romantic works of Mrs Audrey Stone and Marietta Kay Templeton are there in their cheaper editions, and *Murder in Mock Street* and *The Mystery of the Milestone* and *The Casebook of Philippe Plurot*.

'We must not sell the things,' his mother said the day his father died, when Thaddeus was thirteen. They never did. Paintings and furniture continued to be a reminder of the Davenants' heyday: the drawing-room landscapes in tarnished frames, the Egyptian rugs on the wide boards of the floor, the rosewood sofa-table, the white marble of the mantelpiece, Georgian coins. *Rigby, Charing Cross*, the engraving on the carriage clock beneath a glass dome recorded. He would go on being sent away to school, his mother said the day his father died: arrangements had been made for that. Not selling the things, going away to school: all of it was part of something, and the penury must be borne.

'We've talked it over,' comes Mrs Iveson's voice from the hall, and then there is the opening of the hall door, a rasping sound that is particular to it. When his mother died Father Rzadiewicz stayed overnight, and pointed about him at the possessions that had been kept and said that really it was ridiculous not to sell them. Thaddeus agreed, but still did not do so. Instead, as his mother had, he sold the apples and the gooseberries, the pears and plums. He cultivated parsley beds and went in for other herbs, for asparagus and new potatoes, Belle de Fontenay. It was then that he teased back to health the vine in the conservatory. For all his years alone, other people did not come to the house, as they hadn't before: solitude was what he knew and did not fear. 'Yet you have married me in order to be rescued from it,' Letitia pointed out, preferring to believe that.

'Well, that's that, poor little thing.' Returning, Mrs Iveson interrupts these flickers of memory. 'Down in the mouth, I'm afraid.'

'You're really sure about all this?'

Thaddeus doesn't ever address his mother-in-law by name, 'Mrs Iveson' seeming unnecessarily formal, and there has never been an invitation to be more casual in this regard. The question he has asked her is academic; he knows she's sure, and wonders how long it will be before he becomes used to this face across the breakfast table, beauty's remnants in lips that were a rosebud once, in fragile bones beneath well-tended skin, eyes the feature that has not aged. Again he is unnerved, filled with apprehension, and for a single instant he feels that none of this is real, that Letitia has not come back yet on her bicycle, that all that's happening is the nonsense of a dream.

'Yes, I am sure.'

He doesn't want to nod and yet he does, signifying gratitude and finality. Death is mysterious, he finds himself reflecting, in ordering so calmly what life can not. It is a graveyard's gift that a grandmother's rights are sturdier than they were before. Privately rejected when she made it, Letitia's last request will be honoured now: Mrs Ferry will be visited and money paid to her.

3

'A mansion,' Pettie reports. 'He's left with this kid in a mansion.'

Albert's ovoid countenance remains impassive. He nods an acknowledgement in the Soft Rock Café. Pettie says:

'Garages and that.'

As she speaks, the house she has visited becomes vivid for her, as in a photograph: red-brick façade and tall brick chimneys, slender and rounded, spikily decorated; blue paintwork setting off the windows, a blue front door, tarmacadam turn-around, grass and roses and stone steps. The dado of stairway lincrusta – in shiny green – appears, and blue blinds half drawn, softening the sunlight in the diningroom she could see into while she waited in the hall.

There was scarlet-striped wallpaper in the room where the interview took place. There were armchairs in the hall, and a glass door that led to a conservatory full of flowers.

'You get the job, Pettie?' Albert's question is not accompanied by the inflection that indicates interrogation. His voice is toneless, as it invariably is when he is worried, and this morning he is worried about his friend. He smiles to cheer her up, a huge upset in the curve of his features, like an eggshell exploding. Then all expression goes and his eyes are dead again.

Bleakly, Pettie shakes her head. She fishes in a pocket of her short denim skirt for a cigarette, finds two remaining in a crushed packet of Silk Cut and lights one. 'I thought I got it, but I didn't.'

She was dragged all the way out there, but in the end they didn't offer her the job. Quincunx House the place is called, and when Albert asks how they're spelling that she tells him. She tells him which train station she got out at, and how there was a bus journey after that and how she walked up through a village street, not that you could call it a village, with only a shop and a public house and a petrol pump that wasn't working. The other girls were on the train and the bus, three in all. Two of them went into the graveyard by the church, putting in time, and when they finished there she went in herself because she was more than an hour too soon. A grave was new, flowers on the dry earth, but she didn't guess then whose it was. She sat on a railing going round another grave; she read the inscriptions on the stones, the sun beating down on her. Then she went out into the country, along a lane. Miles away, in Essex.

'They didn't take to you, Pettie?'

'They didn't say.'

It could be that they noticed the certificate, but if they did they didn't comment. Years ago, when Pettie first decided to go for child-minding, she borrowed Cassie May's certificate and had it photocopied in a Kall-Kwik with a tab over Cassie May's name. When the tab was peeled off Cassie May didn't know a thing, not even that the certificate had been borrowed.

'No reason why they wouldn't take to you, Pettie.'

'They didn't give no reason.'

Pettie is small, just into her twenties but seeming younger, seeming to be hardly passed out of her childhood. Her shoulders and elbows are sharp, a boniness that's noticeable in her hands and feet. Her face is sharpish also, economically made, without waste. Beneath a narrow forehead trimmed with a sandy fringe, pale-lashed eyes are steady behind their wire-rimmed spectacles, and sometimes taken to be hostile. She could do with a fuller mouth, Pettie considers, and an ounce or two more flesh about the chin, but generally she is content enough: when she makes herself up she considers she can challenge other girls of her age and stature.

'You upset then, Pettie?'

'Yeah.'

She used the typewriter at the Dowlers' to type the reference, scrawling *M. J. Dowler* at the bottom, the back-hand slope of Mrs Dowler's signature reproduced as near's no matter. Not that she knew how to type but she did the best she could; she had to because she knew the Dowlers wouldn't be able to compose a reference, not being the kind of people who know what a reference is. She wasn't asked for one when she started there, which was just as well because the one she got out of the Fennertys wasn't much good, and the people before that refused to give her one because of the necklace business.

'Thaddeus Davenant,' Pettie says, lingering on the syllables. 'The name of that Essex man.'

He gave the full name when she rang up. 'Georgina's father,' he added, and didn't say then there was no mother. Nor did he mention the grandmother who was hanging about, who did the talking at the interview.

'I'm sorry you're upset, Pettie.' Obscuring the brand name of a lager, Albert's chunky hands encircle one of the glass mugs in which tea or coffee is served in the Soft Rock

Café. He smiles again, lending emphasis to this expression of sympathy, and when there's no response he doesn't take offence. He looks around the Soft Rock Café, at its pine tabletops charred here and there where a cigarette has slipped from the edge of an ashtray, its grey metal chairs and unlit juke-box, the two similar posters of a bull and matador, two fruit machines. The red hair of the café's proprietor falls in greasy strands on to the newspaper he is hunched over at the counter. A middle-aged couple do not converse at a table by the door. The deaf and dumb man who spends the greater part of each morning in the café sits where he always sits, with a view of the street.

'You going after another job then, Pettie?'

She's finished with child-minding, Pettie says. She's finished with kids making a bedlam – flour and raisins all over the floor the minute your back's turned, Shredded Wheat floating in the sink, the bedclothes set on fire one time. The morning she typed the reference, Brendan Dowler ate the best part of a packet of Atora. The first day at the Fennertys', Dean put the cat in the fridge. When she walked into the toilet the time Dowler hadn't locked the door he said be my guest.

The house in Essex was a different kind of set-up altogether, you could tell that even before you got there; you could tell from the advertisement, you could tell from the man's voice when she rang up. Living in, the job was, and the minder's room had a carpet and an armchair, dried flowers in a vase, a television. Because of how the man sounded on the phone, giving her directions, saying they were looking forward to seeing her, she was so sure she'd get the job she didn't turn up at the Dowlers' the next morning. Passed on in the Soft Rock Café, this information causes Albert some dismay.

'Don't do to go behind on the rent, Pettie.'

A couple of months ago it was Albert who got Pettie the room in Mrs Biddle's house, across the landing from his own. Mrs Biddle wasn't keen – asserting, in fact, that Pettie frightened her – but in the end she agreed, and Albert feels responsible for the arrangement. Sometimes Pettie is headstrong, not realizing what the consequences of her actions may be. If she doesn't pay the rent she'll have to move on, no way she won't. A tearaway, Mrs Biddle calls her.

'You think about going back to explain to the Dowlers, Pettie? A Saturday today, they wouldn't be at work.'

The time he persuaded her to go back to the Fennertys she said she'd been in a hospital with suspected appendicitis. He was against her saying that, but she argued that she couldn't just tell them she was fed up. Not that any of it mattered: they didn't even listen when she said about the hospital, glad to have anyone for the kids, no matter who.

'Mrs Biddle can't be short on the rent, Pettie. I'm only thinking about that.'

'No way she'll be short.'

'I'm only mentioning it, Pettie.'

Stockily made, two years older than his friend, Albert is a dapper presence in the Soft Rock Café, the three buttons of his brown jacket buttoned, as are the buttons of its matching waistcoat. These clothes have been acquired in a charity shop; his tie and the shirt into which it is tightly knotted were the property of Mrs Biddle's late husband. He wears a watch he sometimes draws attention to, a Zenith, given to him by a couple whose windows he used to clean.

'You hear that name before?' Pettie is saying. 'Thaddeus?'

Albert shakes his head, on which darkish hair is tidily combed and parted. After a moment he says he thinks he has heard the name, but can't remember where. It could have been Miss Rapp in the old days; it could have been a person he was talking to on the street. Fearful of falsehood, as Albert is, he wouldn't like to say.

'The wife was in a photograph.'

And Pettie describes this because it kept catching her eye: a photograph in a silvery frame on a round table with paperweights on it. There were coloured flowers in the glass of the paperweights, and you could tell the photograph was of Thaddeus Davenant's dead wife because it was given pride of place. A road accident was all that was said, which was why a minder for the kid was necessary.

'There's too much speed on them motorways, Pettie.'

Pettie says speed wasn't mentioned. They didn't give a reason, any more than they did for not taking her on, except the grandmother saying they'd changed their minds. The same three girls were waiting for the bus back, and got on to the train. An hour and a half they had to wait in all, longer than the journey itself.

'It's my opinion the old woman done the damage. If he hadn't all but given me the job over the phone I'd not have walked out on the Dowlers, would I? "I'm very sorry," that woman said. You could tell she was lying her face off.'

Albert doesn't comment. Pettie hasn't got the job and that's the end of it. There's no percentage in harping on the house she went all that way out to, or the people she met there. In an effort to change the subject he tells of what he read in a magazine he bought for Mrs Biddle, an account of two interesting coincidences. How a man, having thrown away his mother's purse after he rifled it as a child, saw it forty-one years later in the window of a pawnshop he happened to be passing in another town. How two sisters, separated at birth, identified one another in middle age on a Dutch bus when they were on holiday to see the tulips. Other such cases were recorded in the magazine, and always there was significance in the coincidence, as if what happened was something meant. The worry that had nagged at the man who found his mother's purse was lifted from him when at last he was able to return it, placing in it coins to the value of those he had taken. The sisters who met on the Dutch bus set up house together.

'Oh, yes?' Pettie acknowledges this. She shouldn't have worn the yellow jacket. They'd have seen the state of the covered buttons, they'd have seen the state of the lining when she took it off. The windows that reached down to the floor were open all the time they were in the room because of the warmth, and a big brown dog came padding in and nosed up for a cuddle. The old woman was the grandmother on the wife's side. She had make-up on but you could hardly see it. Soon's she opened her mouth you could tell she was against you.

'She went out of the room to send off the last girl. The only time I was alone with him.'

Her skirt had ridden up a bit because she was sitting on the edge of the sofa, not wanting to be too casual. She pulled it down when she heard the old woman's footsteps coming back, but that wasn't for a few minutes. She smiled at him and he talked to her, even though he was engaged with the dog, patting it. 'He saw me looking at the photo. He nodded, like he could understand what I was thinking.'

Albert listens while the face in the photograph is described. There was fair hair coiled, a dress without a pattern on it, collar turned up. 'Half a smile she had on. Like she was shy.'

'I understand, Pettie.'

'The drawing-room they called the room. He'd have been working in the garden, the clothes he was in.'

When she first walked into the room and he held his hand out for her to shake she noticed it was grimed. 'Georgina's father,' he said, the same way he'd said it on the phone, only this time he didn't give his full name as well. When she was alone with him she kept thinking Thaddeus suited him. The sound of it suited him, his eyes and his face. Thin as a blade he was.

'I said it was sad, his wife and that. I said it, even though the woman was back in the room. "I'll show you the nursery," she said, but I knew it was no good. No chance, I knew. You could tell with that woman.'

Sensing the depth of his friend's disappointment, and fearing it, Albert's unease increases. He knows Pettie well. He knows what Mrs Biddle means when she calls her a tearaway. Another person mightn't use the word, but he knows what's in their landlady's mind.

'He stayed where he was when the grandmother brought me up to the nursery.'

A couple were hanging about on the landing, the man in dark clothes who had opened the front door and a woman with a blue apron over clothes that were dark-coloured too. The man was up a stepladder, doing something to the top

34

of the curtains at a window. The woman was standing with pins in her mouth.

'Well, here's Georgina,' the grandmother said in the nursery, and the baby looked up from a picture painted on the floorboards, blue-eyed, not like her father. The picture was of hills and trees, flowers outside a cottage, sheep on a slope. Lanes wound through ploughed fields and fields of corn or something like it. A railway line was as straight as a die and there were houses and a church, and the Ring o' Bells Inn. Cattle ate hay. There were pigs and chickens in a yard. Horses were looking over a fence.

Albert listens to this description, but none of it means much to him. The streets are what he knows. Once a year there was an outing from the Morning Star home, where he and Pettie were brought up and from which, eventually, they ran away. You saw fields then, all the way to a seaside place where there were slot machines on the promenade, where they all walked in a bunch along the sands and clambered over the shingle, a wind blowing nearly always. Joe Minching drove them in the minibus that was hired for the day from Fulcrum Street Transport. Joe Minching threw his sandwiches to the seagulls, saying he was used to better grub than that.

'Quiet,' Pettie says. 'I never knew a place as quiet.'

It was quiet when she walked up to the front door and in the hall, in the room where the interview was and on the stairs, on the landing even though those two people were there. Albert listens while more details of the nursery are given, but in his mind's eye he sees the playroom at the Morning Star, where there were toys also – train trucks with a wheel gone, limbless dolls, jigsaws with half the pieces missing, anything that other children had finished with. Old armchair cushions were drawn close to the stove that smelt of burning paraffin in winter. Doorless lockers filled one wall. It was here that Marji Laye told how her father and mother were ice-rink skating stars who had put her in a home for the time being, better than carting her about with them all over the world, depriving her of an education. Sylvie talked about parties, someone playing the melodeon, everyone happy until there was a fire and she was the only one left. Bev said her father was in the House of Lords and knew the Queen. But Joe Minching said Sylvie's mother and sisters were on the game and always had been, that Marji Laye was found wandering on a tip, that Bev came in a plastic bag. From the playroom windows you could see Joe Minching's coke shed, and the tall yard doors with the dustbins in a row beside them, straggles of barbed wire trailing round the manhole of the underground tank that used to conserve rainwater in the old days, its missing cover replaced by planks weighed down with concrete blocks.

'Georgina Belle,' Pettie says. 'When I saw her I kept thinking I'd call her Georgina Belle. I'd get the job and I'd call her that. We'd go downstairs and the grandmother would have changed her mind on the way. The way he smiled when he was patting the dog, you could see he's keen.'

'Keen, Pettie?'

'Keen I'd come there is all I mean.'

Albert doesn't respond to that. There's an aeroplane passing over and what he'd like to do is go to see what line it belongs to, to wait for it to come closer and catch the emblem. But this is not the morning for that, and instead he makes another effort at distraction.

'You give that bugle in, Pettie?'

A week ago, when they had left the Soft Rock Café and were walking about, Pettie found a bugle in a supermarket trolley that someone had abandoned in a doorway. She tried to blow it but no sound came, and Albert wasn't successful either. A special skill, a man going by said.

'Yeah, I give it in.'

'Salvation Army property.'

'I give it in at the hostel.'

She took it to a man who buys stuff for car-boot sales, who generally accepts anything she brings him. He said at first the bugle was worthless. In the end he gave her forty pence for it.

'Salvation Army do a good job, Pettie.'

The grandmother took her into the bed-sitting room they'd got ready for the minder. 'Come next door, Nanny,' she said. Why'd the woman bring her in there if they didn't want her? Why'd she bother? Why'd she even bring her upstairs? Why'd she call her that? 'Course she wouldn't change her mind. All the time she was against her.

'I asked at the hostel,' Albert says. 'I said I couldn't play an instrument, but the man said no problem if I wanted to join the Army.'

The couple were moving away from the landing when they passed again, the man carrying the stepladder. 'Wait here a minute, would you?' the grandmother said in the hall. A clock in the panelling ticked and there were voices from behind the closed door, but she couldn't hear what was being said. The voices went on and on, and then the old woman came out. She shook her head. Twice she said she was sorry.

'Best forgotten, Pettie.'

'She give me a ten-pound note for the fare. Ten pounds eighty it cost me.'

'You like I go round and put it to the Dowlers for you?' Another smile lights Albert's eyes, upsetting the composure of his face, crinkling his cheeks and forehead. 'You like I say you made a mistake about the job?'

'The Dowlers are the pits.'

Eight till eight, the arrangement at the Dowlers' was, but more often than not neither parent turned up till ten, with never a penny offered for the extra hours. 'Give them something about six,' Mrs Dowler would say, and there was always a fuss because they didn't like what was in the few tins that were regularly replaced on the kitchen shelves. Dowler fixes people's drains for them, driving about in a van with *Dowler Drains 3-Star Service* on it, a coarse black moustache sprawled all over the lower part of his face. Overweight and pasty-skinned, Mrs Dowler in her traffic-warden's uniform harangues her children whenever she's in their company, shouting at them to get on, shouting at them to be quiet, telling them to wash themselves, not noticing when they don't. 'They had the NSPCC man round,' the woman next door told Pettie once, and Pettie realized then that she was only there because the NSPCC man had ordered Mrs Dowler to get a daytime minder.

'You lend me a few pounds, Albert?'

He counts the money out in small change. He makes stacks of the different coins on the table and watches Pettie scoop them into her purse. Two girls have come into the café and are playing the fruit machines. The lights of the antiquated juke-box have come on. The deaf and dumb man is still in the window, the middle-aged couple still don't speak. The red-haired proprietor turns over a page of his newspaper.

'Fancy the dinosaurs, Pettie?'

He smiles, but when she shakes her head the light goes from his eyes and his features close in disappointment. It was her idea to go to see the dinosaurs in the first place. A million years old, those bones, she said.

'Fancy going out to the Morning Star?'

When they were still there the Morning Star home was condemned as unfit for communal habitation. The inspectors who came round investigated the load-bearing walls, took up floorboards and registered on their meters the extent of damp and rot. A year after Albert and Pettie left they went back to look. *Site for Sale after Demolition*, a notice said. They managed to get in, and still occasionally return to wander about the passages and rooms, Albert showing the way with his torch.

'No, not the Morning Star.' Pettie shakes her head again. 'Not today.'

Albert drinks the last of his milky tea, cold now in the glass mug. She won't be comforted. Sometimes it's as though she doesn't want to be. Her high-heeled shoes are scuffed, her white T-shirt has traces of reddish dye from some other garment on it. He knows from experience that she's in the dumps.

'What you going to do, Pettie?'

'I got to sort myself. I got to go wandering.'

'Down the shops, Pettie? I need a battery myself.'

39

'I got to be on my own today.'

She stands up, telling him he should rest because of his night work. He needs to sleep, she reminds him, everyone needs sleep. Albert works in Underground stations, erasing graffiti when the trains aren't running.

'Yeah, sure,' he says, because it's what she wants. The girls playing the fruit machines move from one to the other, not saying anything, pressing in coins and hoping for more to come out, which sometimes happens.

'Yeah, sure,' Albert says again.

She knows he's worried, about the job, about the rent, maybe even because she has feelings for that man. Not being the full ticket, he worries easily: about cyclists in the traffic, window-cleaners on a building, a policeman's horse one time because it was foaming at the teeth. He worried when they found the bugle, he worried when Birdie Sparrow found a coin on the street outside the Morning Star, making her give it in because it could be valuable and she'd be accused. He said not to take them when the uncles came with their presents on a Sunday, but everyone did. He was the oldest, the tallest although he wasn't tall. The first time he helped Marti Spinks to run off in the night they caught her when it was light, but she never said it was he who had shown her how. The next time she got away, with Merle and Bev. When Pettie's own turn came he said he was coming too because she had no one to go with. 'Best not on your own,' he said, and there wasn't a sound when he reached in the dark for the keys on the kitchen hook, nor when he turned them in the locks and eased the back door open. He didn't flash his torch until they'd passed through the play yard and were half-way down the alley, the long way round to Spaxton Street but better for not being seen, he said. 'Crazy's a bunch of balloons,' Joe Minching used to say, but nobody else said Albert was crazy, only that he wasn't the same as the usual run of people.

'You don't go messing with the Dowlers, Albert. You leave them be.'

'I only wanted to put it to them.'

'You leave them be. Cheers, Albert.'

'Take care now, out there on your own.'

'Yeah, sure.'

As she always does, Pettie buys the cheapest ticket at the Tube station in order to get past the barrier. Two youths on the train keep glancing in her direction. They're the kind who don't pull their legs back when you stand up, obliging you to walk around them: Pettie has experienced that on this line before. Ogling her, one of them holds his hands out, palms facing each other, indicating a length, as a man boasting of a caught fish might. But Pettie knows this has nothing to do with fish. The other youth sniggers.

She looks away. The uncle with the birthmark took off her glasses the first time they were on their own. 'Let's have a look at you,' he said and put the glasses on the window-sill. 'Oh, who's a beauty now?' he said, and when he whispered that he liked her best a warmth spread through her that came back, again and again, whenever he said it.

The youths get off at Bethnal Green. One of them says something but she doesn't hear it, not wanting to. 'Prim little lady,' the uncle who liked her said. 'Who's my prim little princess?' He told her what a cheroot was because he had a packet in his pocket. She was prim and she still is; being prim is what she wants. '*Never so much as a morsel taken*

41

from the knife,' Miss Rapp read out from the *Politely Yours* column. *'Return the fork to the plate between mouthfuls.'* She practised that, and Miss Rapp was pleased.

Aldgate goes by, and Bank; Pettie closes her eyes. Wild summer flowers are in bloom, and it could be the picture on the floor but it isn't because she's in the picture herself. She's in the lane with a buggy, far beyond the few houses by the shop and the petrol pump, far beyond the church and the graveyard and the gateless pillars of the house. She's walking out into the countryside, and fields stretch to the horizon, with the wild flowers in the hedges, a plain brick farmhouse in the distance. 'Look, a rabbit,' she whispers, and Georgina Belle waves at the rabbit from the buggy, and you can smell honey in the honeysuckle.

At Oxford Circus she goes with the crowd, jostled on the pavement. A gang of girls gnaw chicken bones and drink from cans, laughing and shouting at one another, strung out, in everyone's way. Beggars poke out their hands from doorways, tourists dawdle, litter is thrown down. Street vendors sell perfume and watches and mechanical toys. Men in coloured shorts unwrap summer lollipops. Women expose reddened thighs. 'Thaddeus Davenant,' Pettie says aloud.

He ran his fingers along the pale wood that edged the back of the sofa, standing there for a moment before she sat down, the grandmother already occupying a chair. He was solemn, not smiling when she held out the reference and the certificate. Still mourning his loss, he naturally wouldn't have smiles to spare. Something about him reminds her of the man who talked to her in Ikon Floor Coverings, who explained why he recommended 0.35 wearing thickness in a vinyl. Thaddeus Davenant's clothes were nothing like the grey suit and clean white shirt, *Eric* on the badge in the lapel, but there was something about his quiet manner that reminded her. More than once she went back to Ikon Floor Coverings, until the time he wasn't there, gone on to another store, they didn't know where. Not that she wants to think about the floor-coverings man now, nor the Sunday uncle either, since they let her down in the end. 'Oh, yes, a lovely walk,' Pettie says instead, and Thaddeus Davenant takes his tiny daughter from her arms. 'Georgina Belle,' he says.

★

Carefully, Albert attaches the Spookee sticker to his wall. He has all eight of the Spookee stickers now, collected from Mrs Biddle's cornflakes' packets. He stands back a foot or two to inspect the arrangement, his empty eyes engaged in turn with each of the grey, watery creatures, one with a red tongue lolling out, another gnashing devilish teeth. He moves further away, surveying the stickers from the door in order to see what the decoration looks like just in case Mrs Biddle ever glances in, not that she can manage the stairs, but you never know.

Albert looks after Mrs Biddle in return for this room. Years ago, when he and Pettie ran away from the Morning Star, they slept rough, at first in an abandoned seed nursery and after that in cars if they could get into them, or in sheds left unlocked on the allotments that stretched for half a mile behind a depository for wrecked buses. In time Albert heard about the night work on the Underground; he slept by day, on benches or in waiting-rooms. Then, because he happened to be passing, he helped a man with elephantiasis to cross a street and the following morning he noticed the man again and helped him again, this time carrying for him a pair of trousers he was taking to a dry cleaner's.

Albert waited on the pavement outside the cleaner's and when the man emerged he fell into step with him. He felt compassion for the man's suffering – the great bloated body, the moisture of sweat on his forehead and his cheeks, the difficulty he experienced in gripping with his fingers. Albert did not say this but simply walked beside the man, restraining his own natural motion so that it matched the slow drag of the man's. They did not speak much because speech was difficult for the man while he was engaged in the effort of movement, but when they reached a small supermarket – the Late-and-Early KP Minimarket – he thanked Albert for his assistance and his company, and turned to enter the place. He had time to spare, Albert said, and followed him in.

He carried the wire basket around the shelves, filling it as he was directed. The man rested, leaning against the shelves where tins of soup and vegetables were stacked, calling out to Albert the remaining items on his list. A family of Indians ran the minimarket, two young men and their parents, the mother at the till. When the shopping was complete and paid for, Albert took the carrier-bags that contained it and the man did not demur, although when they were on the street again he might have been left standing there. Later, when he and Albert knew one another better, the man mentioned that. It would not have been an unusual occurrence nowadays for a young person to befriend an afflicted man in order to steal from him when the moment was ripe. 'But though I look no more than sawdust in a skin,' the man with elephantiasis stated, 'I can spot an honest face.'

On the morning of the shopping expedition he had led the way to his council accommodation and had invited Albert in when they reached it. He was tired, resting again while Albert, at his instruction, buttered cream crackers and prepared two cups of Bovril. He noticed that the man was not in the habit of washing the dishes he ate from and so, every morning after this one, Albert called in to attend to the chore, to make the Bovril and at one o'clock to open a tin of beans, which they shared on toast, with a banana afterwards. Still unable to afford a place to sleep, his work on the Underground being ill-paid, Albert was grateful for the comfort of the man's rooms, for the armchair that became the one he always sat in, for the warmth and the food. But this convenience was not his motive. He did not seek to cultivate a relationship for profit: it had come naturally to him to assist the man across the street when he recognized signs of stress. It was natural, too, that he should have accompanied him to the Late-and-Early KP Mini-market and should have carried his purchases. Not much thought, certainly no cunning, inspired these actions. *Elephantiasis* Albert wrote down, having asked the man how he was spelling that. He liked the sound of the word; he liked the look of the letters when he wrote them.

One day, arriving as usual on a morning there was to be a visit to the minimarket, Albert was taken aback when his ringing of the doorbell remained unanswered. A neighbour was attracted by his worry as he stood there, and then another neighbour. Something was wrong, they said, and there was excitement when drama was anticipated. A small crowd gathered, a police car arrived, and already the man who did not open his door was spoken of in the past tense. Forcible entry was made; inside, the television screen flickered, an American domestic comedy in progress. Slumped low in his outsize armchair, eyes still and glassy, the man Albert had looked after was no longer alive.

Five days later, at the funeral, Albert met Mrs Biddle when she slipped on the crematorium steps, saving herself by sitting down. Albert was one of several mourners who helped her to her feet and it happened that it was his arm she particularly held on to. There was to be a drink or two in the house next door to the dead man's, since neighbours rather than any family had been his associates for as long as people could remember. 'You'll come on in?' Mrs Biddle invited Albert, and afterwards she asked him to see her safely to where she lived herself, in Appian Terrace, two streets away from the council estate. As he did so, she told him that some days her arthritis was so bad she couldn't move from her bed. She lived in fear of the social services, she confided, constantly apprehensive that they would poke their noses into her life, counsellors they called themselves. *Mrs Biddle* Albert wrote down afterwards, having learnt that this was her name. He perceived a significance in the fact that she had been at the funeral, as previously he had perceived a significance in the fact that he was passing by when the man with elephantiasis wished to cross the street. He cleaned Mrs Biddle's house for her, did her shopping, and was instructed to give the social services a flea in the ear if they arrived on the doorstep. Years ago in the kitchen of the Morning Star home he had learnt how to fry – sausages, bacon, bread, an egg – and something fried was good for her, so Mrs Biddle said. Sometimes, for a change, he brought her a take-away, a curry, chips with a burger, or

chicken from the Kentucky. He made her hot drinks, Oval-
tine or Horlicks, Ribena or Marmite or cocoa, whatever
she was in the mood for. 'I come in for a place,' he passed
on to Pettie. 'There's an old lady give me a room.'

Mrs Biddle says Albert is as a son to her. She would prefer
it if he didn't go out every night, but he has pointed out
that cleaning up the Underground is work that has to be
done. He is fortunate to have the work, he explains, a stroke
of good fortune come his way.

'You OK then, Mrs Biddle?' he inquires after he has
stuck up the Spookee stickers. 'You manage to eat a bit?'

Mrs Biddle has eaten everything. In the sitting-room
where she also sleeps she is still in bed, watching television,
a game show with numbered boxes. She turns it off because when Albert is there she likes to hear his news.

'Yeah, I been down the shops,' he answers when she asks.
'I paid the gas.'

'You get the woman with the hair?'

'Yeah, I got her. Violet she's called. She has it on her
badge.'

'I wouldn't be surprised what she's called, that woman.'

Albert says it takes all sorts. He stacks the dishes Mrs
Biddle has eaten from, making room on a tray for the metal
teapot she has herself carried to her room. For a moment
he worries, reminded by the teapot of her picking her
steps from the kitchen, shuffling dangerously along, the teapot's handle wrapped in a cloth where the black plastic
binding fell off years ago. A trip and she could be scalded,
lying there while he's out or asleep. But when Mrs Biddle
decides to make her own tea she will not be moved from
doing so.

'No hurry on them dishes. Rest in the chair, Albert. Keep me company a bit.'

Even more than hearing Albert's news Mrs Biddle likes to share with him the memories that keep her going when she's alone. As Gracie de Lisle, girl assistant to Halriati the Sicilian, and before that as one of the four Singing Cowslips, she has not been unknown. When Mr Biddle married her she was professionally engaged, twice nightly at the Tottenham Grand Empire.

In the small, crowded room – rows of cottages on shelves and in cabinets, camels and elephants and reindeer on the mantelpiece – Albert hears further highlights from the theatres and the halls. The cottages are of china, dully glazed so that a sense of reality is retained; the animals are of a brown material that has been grained to resemble carved wood. Theatrical photographs are displayed in mock-wooden frames on two tables and on the walls.

'Nineteen forty-eight, the old Hip in Huddersfield. *Puss in Boots* and the lights failed.'

'What did you do, Mrs Biddle?' Albert asks, although he knows.

'Candles we had to resort to, the usherettes' flashlights, you name it we had it. The day after Boxing Day. Spoilt it for the kiddies, they said.'

Albert never minds hearing a highlight more than once, throwing in the odd response in order to keep company with her because it's company she's after. He stayed with her all day the time her front-garden ornaments disappeared, and again when the social services wrote about her pension, saying it could be reduced, and again when they sent a request to know when it was she'd died. Keeping company is the heart of looking after people, as Albert first experienced in his Morning Star days. 'Stay by me, Albert,' they used to say, a catchphrase it became. The time the youths laughed when the man with elephantiasis sat down to rest himself on the edge of the pavement he stayed with him until the youths went away, even though the man said he was used to abuse on the streets.

'"Milk that cow!" Aubrey shouted from the stilts, and then the back kicked the bucket away and the front did the little dance that had them in stitches. Harry Sunders was the best back in the business. Clowny took the front, and those two always had strong beer in the cow. A couple of Stingos in their pockets and sometimes they spilt it. Brought the house down when the Stingo dribbled out. They'd be prancing about, not knowing they was leaving little pools.'

'Yes,' Albert says. Everything is on the tray now. He tidies the bed, gathering up pages of the local newspaper and a magazine, listening to further tales while he does so. When there's a pause he says:

'You know you can be in the Salvation Army without musical knowledge, Mrs Biddle?'

Mrs Biddle sniffs. Peculiar in this day and age, the Salvationists. Grown men and women with their tambourines. Dismissively, she shakes her head. She could do without the Salvationists this morning.

'You hear of Joseph of Arimathea, Mrs Biddle?'

Mrs Biddle doesn't know if she has heard of Joseph of Arimathea or not. There was Joseph and Dan Saul, kept a greengrocer's, Jewish boys. The father was a Joseph, too. The family moved up West, Dan Saul went into jewellery. Flashy he always was.

'Time of Jesus, Joseph of Arimathea. He took the body. There was another bloke come down out of a tree and carries the Cross. The time the Army was preaching I went up to them and asked the one with the glasses how they're spelling Arimathea.'

Albert spells it now. Arimathea was a place, he explains, a desert locality, not so much as a bush to shade the ground. No water, nothing. Put seeds down and they wouldn't grow.

You can't live without water, Mrs Biddle tetchily agrees, anyone living there should have moved away. Street preachers will tell you anything, Adam and Eve, feed the multitude with a fish. 'Anything comes into their heads and then they get the tambourines out.'

'They didn't have no tambourines the day I asked the man, Mrs Biddle. In their lunch hour it was.'

'Same difference to me, Albert. All that about a burning bush, all that about a star. They lull you with the music.'

Albert doesn't protest further. He collects a cup and saucer he hasn't noticed on the window-ledge. Mrs Biddle says there's trouble with the Lottery.

'Some man strung himself up. Win the Lottery and it's the end of you, the new thing is.'

Albert asks about that, picking up the tray. It could be you have to pay for the uniform. Stands to reason, the Army couldn't go handing out clothes. Albert understands that, but doesn't say so now because her attention wanders whenever he mentions the Army – the way it does when he says SAS or Air India has just gone over, or when he tries to tell her about Joey Ells. The time he told her about scratching his initials on the brick under the windowsill at the Morning Star she fell asleep.

'A couple of thousand you'd get in the Irish Sweep. Enough for anyone.'

''Course it is, Mrs Biddle.'

Twice he put his initials there, *A. L.*, and the year, *1983*. It was Mrs Hoates who told him his other name was Luffe, something he hadn't known. She'd chosen Luffe because it suited him, she said. Albert Luffe. She spelt it for him when he asked and he wrote it down.

'Get us a curry later on, Albert? Something from Ishi Baba's?'

Albert holds the tray with one hand while he opens the door. No problem about a curry. He'll have a sleep and then he'll see what's on offer.

'You know what I'd like, Albert?'

'What's that then?'

'You make me a jelly, Albert? You make me a jelly and put it in the ice compartment for tonight?'

He nods, and Mrs Biddle declares that with a jelly to look forward to she'll get up. She'll get up and she'll catch the afternoon sun by the window. Then there'll maybe be something on the TV. A load of rubbish, that show with the boxes was, the man's clothes too tight on him.

'Good for you to get up.' Albert repeats what a woman in the KP told him when he reported that sometimes he has difficulty persuading Mrs Biddle to leave her bed. Bedsores there could be, apparently. Joints seizing up if you lay there.

'You got a red jelly at all, Albert?'

'Yeah, I got one.'

The Morning Star has come into his mind because of

remembering the initials. Miss Rapp in the mornings with 'O Kind Creator', her fingers dashing along the piano keys. Mrs Cavey on her hands and knees in the bootroom, red polish on a hairbrush. Plaster falls from the stairway wall, the smell of boiling cabbage creeps upstairs. The cars come on a Sunday, the coats hang on the hallstand, big heavy coats worn to Rotary and to church, dark hats on the curved pegs, the uncles' gloves on the shelf below the mirror. Johneen Bale was given a dress and socks an uncle's children had grown out of, Leeroy a bottle-opener, the mongol girl a bangle she sold to Ange, Ahzar and Little Mister frisbees. Cakes and jamrolls there were, beads and rings and plastic puzzles: he found the places to hide when they didn't want to take the presents any more. 'Don't bother me now, boy,' Mr Hoates said every time he tried to tell, Mr Hoates gone sleepy, his hour of Sunday rest, his gas fire hissing. Mrs Cavey said wash your mouth out. 'Stay by me, Albert,' Joey Ells begged, but he couldn't that time and she hid in the rainwater tank, crawling under the strands of barbed wire, making a gap in the planks that covered the manhole. 'Who's seen Joey Ells?' Mr Hoates asked at Sunday tea and someone said there was snow on the ground, there'd be her footprints. 'Shine your torch down, Albert,' Mr Hoates said, and she was there with her legs broken. Mrs Hoates went visiting on a Sunday afternoon, when the uncles came. 'Now, what d'you want to do that for?' she said to Joey Ells when she returned. 'Frightening the life out of us.'

In the kitchen Albert washes up. The Chicken Madras is always the preference from Ishi Baba's. He doesn't mind himself, the Chicken Madras or the beef, whatever's on. He separates the squares of a Chivers' strawberry jelly and when the water on the gas jet boils he pours it on to them, stirring until they dissolve.

No way will Pettie have money for the rent if she doesn't go back to the Dowlers or start in somewhere else. Come Friday there'll be the knocking on the ceiling with the walking-stick and Mrs Biddle saying she's not a charity. She never wanted that girl in the house in the first place, she'll remind him, which from time to time she does anyway, rent or no rent. It rouses her suspicion that Pettie keeps a low profile in the house, hardly making a sound on the stairs or when she opens the front door or closes it behind her. Claiming that the sitting-room has a smell, she never looks in for a chat with Mrs Biddle. It worries Albert that she won't be able to find other employment and will make for the streets where Marti Spinks and Ange hang about, where Little Mister's with the rent boys. 'Don't ever go up Wharfdale,' he has warned her often enough, but sometimes she doesn't answer.

Finding room for the jelly among packets of frozen peas and potato chips in the refrigerator, Albert's concern for Pettie gathers vigour. She won't be able to give him back the money she borrowed, and when he asks her what she's doing for work she won't say. She'll sit there in the Soft Rock, making butterflies out of the see-through wrap of a cigarette packet or tapping her fingers if the music is on, not hearing what's said to her because of this house she has been to. He'll say again that he should go round to the Dowlers to try to get the job back. The chances are she won't answer.

A fluffy grey cat crawls along the windowsill, pausing to look in at him. Albert doesn't like that cat. Closing the refrigerator door, and catching sight of the animal again as he turns around, he remembers how it once jumped down from the opening at the top of Mrs Biddle's window and landed on her pillow, terrifying her because she was asleep. The cat is another worry Albert has, though nothing like as nagging a one as his worry about Pettie. As if it knows this and is resentful, it mews at Albert through the glass, displaying its pointed teeth. There's a cat that goes for postmen's fingers when they push the letters into the box, vicious as a tiger, a postman told him.

The mewing ceases and Albert is spat at. Claws slither on the window-pane, the fluffy grey tail thrashes the air, and then the creature's gone. It'll be the end of her if Pettie goes up Wharfdale, same's it was for Bev.

★

At a scarf counter she unfolds scarves she can't afford to buy, trying some of them on. Busy with another customer, the sales assistant isn't young, a grey, bent woman whom Pettie feels sorry for: awful to be on your feet like that all day long, at the beck and call of anyone who cares to summon you, forever folding the garments that have been mussed up.

In the coat department the assistant is younger, a black girl with a smile. She keeps repeating that the blue with the bows at the collar suits Pettie, and brings her a yellow and a green of the same cut. ''Course the bows slip on and off, you have what colour bow you want,' the black girl points out, and Pettie is reminded of Sharon Lite, who had to have electric-shock treatment years afterwards. Albert occasionally comes across someone from the home, someone who recognizes him on the street or in an Underground, who passes on bits of news like that. 'No, sorry,' Pettie apologizes, and the black girl says she's welcome.

In a shoe shop she tries on shoes, fifteen pairs in all. She walks about with a different shoe on either foot. She asks for half a size larger and begins again. She asks about sandals, but sandals are scarce at the moment, she's told, everyone after them. She examines the tights on a rack by the doors and leaves the shop with a pair of navy blue and a pair of taupe. No way you can walk out of a store with a coat, but at least she has a scarf with horses' heads on it, and a blue bow and a silvery one, and the tights.

On the street again she examines spectacles in an optician's window. All of them are more attractive than hers. She saw the grandmother looking at hers, not thinking much of them. 'No, I don't think so,' the grandmother would have said to him behind that closed door, and he'd have argued that he didn't see why not. But the grandmother would have gone on and on.

'Of course, you could go for contacts,' the woman in the optician's suggests, although she's wearing glasses herself, with jewels in the hinge area and silver trim on the side pieces. Disposable contact lenses you can have now, she points out, no more than a film over the eyes, throw them away every night. Available on EasiPlan, the woman says.

'How much, though?' Pettie asks, and there are questions then, and calculations, and a form to fill in, information required about the applicant's bank account, name and address of employer, length of time in present position, if credit has ever been refused or withheld. Pettie says she'll think about it. The scarf with the horses' heads on it is draped over a pair of smoky blue frames which Pettie is about to take into her possession. But she can tell that the woman with the jewelled hinges is sharp, and changes her mind.

'Excuse me, please.'

For a moment she imagines the man outside the optician's is a detective who has followed her from the scarf counter or the shoe shop, but when he speaks again it is to ask the way to Marble Arch. Pettie directs him, repeating the directions because he isn't quick on the uptake. When she has finished and has told him how long she estimates the journey will take on foot, which is how he has indicated he intends to make it, he invites her to have a cup of tea or coffee. 'Maybe stronger?' he offers also. He's sallow-skinned, from somewhere in the East, Pettie speculates. Beer? he suggests, still smiling. Maybe barley wine, which bucks you up?

Pettie walks away. In Leicester Square she sits at the end of a damp wooden seat otherwise occupied by a couple fondling one another. There was a smell of lavender when she was waiting in the hall, maybe coming from the polish on the panelling because you could smell a waxiness, too. There was a gong like the one the slave hits at the beginning of old films, only smaller, and through an open door she could see the dining-room silver – little ornamental fowls on a big oval table, and salt and pepper containers – and blue glasses on a sideboard, and a fireguard that was a seat as well, upholstered in red leather and buttoned. The silver was valuable, anyone could tell that. One of the fowls would have gone into her bag so's you'd hardly notice the bulge, spoons from the sideboard, a little china box from the table in the hall. But she didn't even consider it.

The couple who have been fondling one another go away. She took her glasses off when the grandmother was out of the room. She held them for a minute, wanting him to see her without them, but unable to see him properly herself. 'I hope you didn't find the journey too terrible,' he said, and she shook her head; the journey was nothing. 'There would be adequate time off,' he'd said on the phone. 'We could arrange that between us.' He had made his mind up then. He had made his choice; he was a man who knew immediately. Time off she would spend in the garden or just walking about the country, not ever bothering to go back to the streets. She would have told him that if the grandmother hadn't come back then.

A black man, talking, sits down where the couple were. He scatters crumbs for the pigeons, breaking up bread he takes from a pocket. He is speaking about someone for whom he would lay down his life or obtain money by whatever means. His eyes are bloodshot, his teeth flash as he converses, seeming occasionally to address the pigeons, who softly coo for him. Two women go by, talking about their health.

It was just before the old woman said they'd go upstairs to the nursery that she knew she definitely had feelings for him. She looked back from the door and he was stroking the dog again, a consolation in his hurting. That grave would have been in his mind, and his motherless baby.

It has helped, going round the shops: it's nice to think of the scarf in her handbag, and the bows from the coats, and the tights. If she'd walked out of the optician's with the smoky frames she would have had to find out in another shop if she could replace her wire ones with them, which would cost her – some exorbitant amount, as always is the case when you want something. Tuesday or Wednesday she'll take what she's got to the car-boot man, with a few more items added in the meantime. No point in going out there with only three.

Taking possession of things touches a part of Pettie she does not understand, stirring an excitement in her that never fails to brighten up the day. The first time she did it in a shop – her fingers edging towards a blue ballpoint pen – she experienced a throb of fear and hesitated, thinking she couldn't. Yet a moment later she did. 'No, over to the right,' she instructed the man behind the counter, who had to stand on a stool to reach a box of chocolates with a castle on it. Her fingers drew the ballpoint towards her, then closed around it. A bigger box was what she was after, she said, and flowers she'd prefer to a castle. Outside, she threw the ballpoint away.

The car-boot man approached her one day when she'd just come out of a shop. If ever she had anything she wanted to get rid of – articles of clothing she had tired of, odds and ends she might dispose of – he'd give her a good price, old or new, it didn't matter. She went with him to his house and spread out on a table what she had just acquired. He didn't pay much in spite of what he'd said about a good price, and never has on any of the occasions she has visited him since. He makes an offer, take it or leave it; the best he can do, times are hard. Bearded, with glasses, he has never revealed his name. His house is stuffy, the windows always tightly closed. The money he pays her comes from odd jobs, she tells Albert, who always wants to know where money comes from. Cleaning, she says. Working a price-gun.

'No, man. No more.' The last of the black man's crumbs have been scattered, but the pigeons still crowd his legs.

Two weeks he has gone without a drink, he assures the pigeons and the companion who is not present. 'Honey, that is for you. Honey, I suffer.'

People wait outside the cinemas, drab against the glamour of the posters and the familiar faces of the stars. Georgina Belle could be a star's name, and Pettie wonders how it came into her thoughts. 'A total waste that was,' a cross voice complains, and a couple walk away.

The grandmother said they'd only minutes ago decided on another arrangement. She would be coming to live in the house herself, to take her daughter's place as best she could until the baby was older. It was sensible in the circumstances, but Pettie didn't listen to why that was. The clock in the panelling struck, five o'clock it would have been. The grandmother said something about the heatwave when she held the front door open, then gave her the ten-pound note.

In a Wimpy Bar Pettie squirts tomato ketchup on to chips and grey minced meat. *When out to dinner,* Miss Rapp's column laid down, *refrain from recounting the details of a hospital operation while other folk are eating*. You'd get into the way of things in a house like that one. You'd leave something for Miss Manners, you'd get your grammar right. Blush pink on your fingernails, nothing objectionable, nothing the woman holding the stepladder could sniff at. Magic Touch on any skin defects.

Her Coca-Cola comes. She sips a little, then slowly begins to eat, not registering the taste, nor where she is. She lights her remaining cigarette and crumples up the empty packet. 'Come downstairs for a sherry,' he invites, his quiet baby asleep, a rag doll on the pillow. The sherry glasses have long stems, two glasses on a red and gold tray. 'It suits you, Nanny,' he says, about the uniform they have given her. Two shades of blue, with only touches of white, the stockings black. A widower is lonely: that's there between them. He doesn't say it; he doesn't have to; the old woman couldn't manage it is what he says, too much for her. It's dark outside, a winter's evening and the fire is lit.

4

Six days go by and then Thaddeus does what he feels he has to, having put it off, but now wanting to get it over. He has been given a time and a place, four o'clock in the Tea Cosy. He brings with him fifty pounds in notes.

The teashop is in the town where Mrs Ferry was once the receptionist at the Beech Trees Hotel. The Beech Trees has gone, and with it Mrs Ferry's onetime husband, whom she would settle for now. She lives alone, in a room above a confectioner's. The Tea Cosy is in a busier street, five minutes away.

'Bad Hat!' Mrs Ferry exclaims from where she sits when Thaddeus enters, lowering his head beneath the beam with a sign on it to warn him. *Bad Hat!* her Valentine message ran seventeen years ago, among others in a local paper. *But good for his ever-loving Dot!*

She has ordered tea, and a plate of cakes, which she was always partial to and used to say she shouldn't be. She bulges out of a spotted yellow dress, a hat reminiscent of a turban hiding much of her henna hair, her lipstick a splash of crimson. Coloured beads lollop over double chins and reach an artificially deepened cleavage, exposed between mammoth breasts. There is no sign in this spectacle of the ill-health so regularly touched upon in Mrs Ferry's letters. Only her weight would seem to be a subject for a consulting room.

'Hullo,' Thaddeus greets his afternoon woman of long ago, recalling her underclothes on the back of a chair, the curtains pulled over. 'Hullo, Dot.'

'Well, dear, you haven't changed. He'll have put on a year or two, I said, but truth to tell you hardly have.'

He smiles, wiping away with his fingers the lipstick she has left on his cheek, which would have been his mouth if she'd had her way. She pours his tea, remarking that, after all, it wasn't yesterday. She speaks in a hurried gabble, doing her best to be lighthearted. She offers Thaddeus the plate of cakes.

'I have to explain,' he interrupts when there's a chance.

But she hurries on, as if fearful of what might be said. 'We've had good times, dear. Don't think I didn't appreciate that. I lie alone in my little place, watching the light come at the curtains, and I think how good the times were. I haven't been well, you know.'

'You said. I'm sorry.'

'I wouldn't have asked another living soul. I lie there remembering our times and I think there's no one I can ask except my old Bad Hat.'

He wishes she wouldn't call him that, but of course it is her right and once he didn't mind. *Thad dear*, her letters have begun: that, also, he didn't mind.

'I've come over because of something that has happened. I didn't send anything before—'

'Shh now, dear.'

'I'm sorry.' He lowers his voice. 'I didn't send anything before because strictly speaking the money's my wife's. I didn't feel I could.' He pauses until her cup is raised, and hurries on while she sips her tea, spreading another red smudge on the china surface. 'But then my wife came across one of your letters.'

'Oh, my God!' Careless herself now, Mrs Ferry causes people to look their way. 'Oh, my dear God!'

Thaddeus doesn't give the details of how the letter came to light. 'It upset her that you were in need. When she read about it she wanted you to have something.'

'I don't believe I follow this, dear.'

Thaddeus does not intend to disclose the fact of his widowhood, feeling that in the circumstances it would not be sensible to do so. He has respected Letitia's wishes, he'll send whatever is demanded in the future, but the consequences of divulging that he is again on his own are very much to be avoided.

'My wife simply wanted to help you. She read your letter and was upset.'

'I'm to blame for a commotion!' is Mrs Ferry's response, declared in the same noisy manner.

'No, no, of course you're not.'

She shakes her head. A shock, she says; she nearly fainted. Her eyes seem smaller than they were a moment ago. Her mouth remains slightly open when she has finished speaking, the tip of her pink tongue revealed.

'I wanted to explain, Dot. I'm very sorry you got a shock.'

'I never meant harm, dear.' Though stated more quietly, a degree of Mrs Ferry's natural perkiness has returned. 'No one wants that. You believe me, dear, no harm was meant?'

'Of course I do.'

'Another fact is, there was nothing any time I wrote to you that was an indiscretion. We have had our indiscretions, not that I regret them, not a single one. But nothing was written by me that could have offended a wife, for I said to myself I must not do that. I wrote when I was at my lowest. The first time I was at my lowest, the next time not so bad but still not able for things. I'm ailing through and through, to tell you the honest truth. Now that you've been kind enough to come over I can say that.'

She lives like this, Thaddeus finds himself reflecting. She writes men begging letters without threats, needling their guilt, sniffing out money. God knows how many overnight commercial travellers have benefited in the past at the Beech Trees. God knows how often the handwriting that slopes in all directions succeeds in eliciting assistance, with muttered oaths.

'I have no money of my own, Dot.'

'You never had, love.'

'I think I tried to explain when you wrote the first time that it felt wrong to give you my wife's money, but I don't think I succeeded.'

'Isn't it strange how things pan out? I was well set up, married to a prosperous man, you hadn't a bean. I didn't want presents, it never mattered.'

She unlocked the door of Room Twenty when the chambermaids had gone home. He went up the back staircase and waited for her, and sometimes – if it was easy – she came with two drinks on a tray, gin and Martini. He used to smoke in those days, but she never let him in Room Twenty because the smell of cigarettes would be a giveaway when the evening maid came on. She didn't want talk in the hotel. She was particular about that.

'I wouldn't have written unless I was down.'

'I know. I understand that.'

'Do you, Thad? Do you really? Do you know what it is to be down?'

'Yes, I do.'

'And short when you're getting on a bit? You weren't much more than a boy when you were selling your garden produce. Oh, how I remember that!'

He filled the van with what he grew or picked from the fruit trees, and set off in the early morning. He supplied Fruit 'n' Flowers on the way and then the Beech Trees, and she was in and out of the kitchen. A grey A30 the van was, second-hand and hardly big enough.

'I was always surprised, you know, you didn't have a job.'

'It was a job of a kind.'

'Oh, heavens, yes. Anyone could see you worked. I often wish we could turn the clock back, Thad. She's younger, is she?'

'A few years.'

'I must have guessed it. You wouldn't have written that.'

'No, I don't think I did.'

'You only wrote back to me the once, dear.'

'All I could have kept on saying was that the money wasn't really mine to give away.'

'Money, money! What a curse it is! Extraordinary, a wife not minding though. You have to say extraordinary, Thad?'

'Yes, it is.'

'Well, there you go, as they say these days.'

'Yes.'

'I hate them, really, these new expressions.'

'Yes.'

'I'm all right, you know. Except for being short I'm all right. I take pills. I've got a few things wrong inside, you know, but there you are. Worse at the moment is the heat. You relish the heat, Thad?'

'Yes, actually I do.'

'You're weather-beaten. It suits you. I wonder if he'll be weather-beaten? I said. He's an outside man, I said, stands to reason it'll show. D'you know what I'd like? I'd like to show you my little place.'

'Oh, look, I don't think—'

'Old times' sake, Thad. Five minutes for old times' sake. I'd love to show you.' And Mrs Ferry whispers, grimacing to make a joke of her reservation: 'I wouldn't want anything handed over here, dear.'

The bill comes swiftly. He pays it and stands up. She gathers together her belongings.

'You haven't lost your looks, Thad.' She lowers her voice again for that, working a dimple, the way she used to. 'A dear, dear friend,' she whispers to a couple who nod to her as they go by, who examine Thaddeus with curiosity. 'Oh, darling, I've mislaid a glove!' she cries, and people at the nearby tables stand up to poke about on the floor for a lace glove, of sentimental value. 'Oh, I'm so fussed today!' Mrs Ferry apologizes when it's discovered in the pocket of her skirt, and the Tea Cosy settles down again.

Two pounds and fourpence arrive in change. Thaddeus reaches for the coins and leaves a tip. With a plastic butcher's bag, the *Daily Telegraph* and the *Radio Times*, her lace gloves in place, a large velvet handbag held tightly, Mrs Ferry is ready now, and on the street outside she takes his arm.

'That's never your car, dear!' she exclaims, eyeing Thaddeus's battered old Saab and Rosie in it. 'Well, I never!'

'Are you far? Is it worth driving?'

'A minute's walk. You have a dog, dear.'

'Yes.'

'Remember the Sealyham at the hotel?'

'Yes, I do.'

'He died, of course. We buried him at the back. Remember Oscar? The daytime porter?'

'Yes, I do.'

'He went a fortnight later, poor old Oscar.'

She opens a door beside a shop window full of jars of sweets, Rolo and Kit-Kat and Mars bars advertised, Easter eggs reduced. The hall they pass through to reach uncarpeted stairs is stacked with cartons of similar confectionery, and strewn with junk mail. People listen in the Tea Cosy, Mrs Ferry explains, they listen and they watch, he probably noticed. In the room she lives in she pours out gin, not offering it first. Both glasses have lipstick on them.

'I haven't changed my tipple.' Mrs Ferry winks, adding the Martini. There should be lemon, she apologizes, there should be ice. But lemons are a price these days, and ice she can never manage, the fridge she has. A fluffy teddybear, in blue with one eye gone, is on the bed.

'Cheers, dear.'

'I must be careful. I have to drive.'

'Poor Oscar went in the hall. He carried in a couple's bags, the next thing was we were loosening the poor chap's collar. "I'll sit down just a minute," he said. Well, truth to tell, that was the end.'

Thaddeus nods, remembering Oscar, old even in 1979, burly and genial. He always suspected that Oscar knew.

'Your mother wasn't long gone in our day, dear. You used to mention your mother the odd time.'

67

'Did I? I don't remember that.'

'Oh, definitely. On the strange side, I considered, but of course I never said. One's nervous, young. A foreign lady, wasn't she?'

'My mother was Polish.'

'Romantic, it sounded. Not that you'd ever say much.'

He never had; he never did. His childhood in that threadbare past is one of shame: his unwanted presence, his garden friendship with the ghosts of pets, footsteps that passed by when he lay awake, whispers on the stairs.

'Close you were, dear. Oh, very close.'

'I suppose I was.'

He takes two twenty-pound notes and a ten from his wallet and places them on a bamboo table. He can see her counting them from a distance. He tells her how much is there.

'Butter side up you've landed, dear. I haven't done so well myself. What's she like?'

'I don't really want to talk about Letitia.'

'I know, dear, I know. I always thought you'd end up with a smasher, I bet she's that. An eye for the ladies, Chef used to say when you hawked your produce in the Trees.'

He smiles, but it isn't enough. He knows what Mrs Ferry is thinking because it's there in her eyes. It was there in the teashop, it was there when she embraced him: she was his fancy woman, and now he's gone stuffy on her. 'He can be so blooming stuffy,' she used to say, referring to her husband. 'He gets my goat sometimes.'

'Palpitations is what I suffer mainly,' she's saying now. 'A warning, they give it as, and then there's the digestive thing.

I've had more barium meals than a cat's had mice, and still it's a bewilderment to the medics.'

'I'm sorry, Dot.'

'You were romantic yourself, you know, left alone in your big old house. I'd think of you, and long to be there with you. Oh, others did too, I don't delude myself. What was she called, that girl you had before you and I had our naughtiness? Beatrice? Beryl?'

'Bertranda.'

'Funny, that, I always thought. You're still seeing Bertranda, dear?'

'I haven't seen Bertranda since 1977.'

'Well, there you go. Not that I ever knew the girl, but everything's of interest as you get older. You find that, Thad?'

'Not really.'

'You spent a night at the Trees. When his Cheltenham uncle died. Remember that? You had to skulk about, Twenty not being *en suite*.'

Thaddeus doesn't want to remember, but images and sounds occur: the narrow corridor, shoes outside the doors, the lavatory with the cracked window-pane, someone having a bath, a radio on in a room he passed.

'You parked the van two streets away.'

'Yes, I did.'

'That same chef's in the Royal now. We still keep up.'

'I must be going, Dot.'

'Oh, love, you've only just come.' She stands with a bottle in each hand. Old times' sake, she says again. Old times, old flames. A laugh comes moistly, a giggle that rises from some depth within her. The flesh of her chins and of her propped-up breasts wobbles, then settles again. 'Remember that first afternoon, eh? My, you were keen that first afternoon!'

That was long ago, Thaddeus says, then realizes this sounds dismissive. Friendships belong to their time: he corrects his remark in an effort to mend matters. But the effort is wasted because Mrs Ferry still isn't listening.

'Not that I wasn't keen myself, dear. I'm not saying that for a minute. Bucketing down it was. That gutter leaking above the window, drip, drip, drip. I told him afterwards – the gutter above Number Twenty, and he said he'd get Oscar up a ladder.'

'I really must go now.'

'I treated him badly, Thad.' Idly she caresses the blue teddybear, prodding at the empty eye. 'He worshipped me and I threw it back at him.'

'I'm sure you didn't.'

'Poor little man, he wore that cravat to give himself a presence, like he tried for with the moustache. Everything for me, he said, and I threw it back. I lie awake sometimes.'

'I'm sorry.'

'He married again, of course. Happy as a sandboy.'

'Well, that's something.'

'Not for me it isn't, dear. Not for an erring lady. D'you ever think of that, Thad? The error of our ways?'

Thaddeus smiles. He confesses that he often dwells on the error of his ways. He comments on the room they're in, saying it's charming.

'It's what I can afford, dear.' She carries his eyes with hers around the room's contents – the big refrigerator in a corner, the screen that half obscures a sink, the tattered curtains, the television on a shelf, her shopping thrown on to the bed. The evening sun shows up the dust on surfaces. 'The lav's a flight up. She charges for a bath, fifty p on the gas. Oh well, there you are! I soldier on.'

'Yes, you do.'

'You bring that Bertranda to your house, Thad?'

'No, I never did.'

'You can't not bring a wife, though. You let her in, eh?'

'Yes, of course.'

'I'd dearly love to know what she's like. A wife that'd pay good money to an erring lady is never usual, Thad.'

'Look –'

'I understand, dear. Silly to be curious.'

'It doesn't matter.'

'I'd never bother you, Thad. I'd never be a leech.'

She pours more gin and tries to fill his glass as well, but he puts his hand over the top of it. Her husband's in Lytham St Annes, she says, the brass buttons of his blazer still smart, although of course the blazer would be a different one these days, but she can see him in it and she often does, navy blue as ever it was, pen and propelling pencil in the inside pocket, the neat knot of his Paisley tie.

'How well I knew him, Thad!'

'Yes.'

'Not for me the past's been buried. Not long ago or any time, unfortunately.'

Tears run through the powder on her face, thin rivulets wreaking minor havoc. She promised herself she wouldn't, she cries with shrill determination. She swore before he came that not a single tear would fall. 'Bad Hat,' she murmurs, trying for a smile, forcing out a laugh instead. 'My own Bad Hat.'

'I hope it'll be a help.' He nods towards the bamboo table, the notes still where he placed them.

'I have my pride, dear.'

'Yes, of course.'

'She's a – what's her name, Thad?'

'Letitia.'

'That's lovely, dear. A younger wife, no more than a girl, is she? And kiddies too?'

'I have a daughter.'

'I'm truly glad for you. A Sagittarian, Letitia is?'

'A what?'

'I thought you said a Sagittarian. When's Letitia's birthday, dear?'

'May.'

'More like a Gemini, I'd say. And what's the little daughter called, dear?'

'Georgina.'

'Five? Six?'

'Georgina'll be six months in a few weeks.'

'Capricorn, I shouldn't wonder. And you're Aquarius yourself, as I remember.'

'I must go, Dot.'

'Remember, I'd say you were always going? A shadow flitting?'

'Yes, I remember.'

He touches a cheek with his lips and feels it damp. A hand grasps one of his, her body presses, thighs and knees, mouth searching, and suddenly her tongue. The rim of the glass she still holds is sharp on his stomach, its contents spilling into his shirt.

'Oh, darling, I'm sorry!'

She fusses with a handkerchief, dabbing him with it. He can't go yet, she insists, and disappears behind the screen. She runs a tap and squirts out washing-up liquid. It doesn't matter, Thaddeus protests, but she says it does, wiping him with a soapy cloth.

'Whatever'll she say? Whatever'll she think you've been up to, dear?'

'It's all right. Please don't worry.'

'Be honest with me, Thad: she didn't think harassment when she read the letter?'

'Harassment?'

'It's what they call it these days. Privacy invaded when all there's been is a few letters. You tell her no harm meant. You tell her that?'

'Yes, of course.'

'Forgive me for all this kerfuffle, dear.'

'Of course I do.'

'You won't forget old Dot?'

'Of course I won't.'

He looks back from the door before he goes. The wet cloth is on the bed beside her, she has poured herself another drink. She hugs her teddybear, trying to smile again. She raises her glass to him.

'I loved you all over again this afternoon, Thad.'

He smiles away this protestation, shaking his head. In the past she wasn't a drunk. She held the aces, as she used to say; she could have had anyone. Brash and shiny, irresistible on a barstool, or suddenly in the kitchen when he delivered what the chef she still keeps up with had ordered, there was an extraordinary excitement about her until she threw him over for an insurance salesman. 'Why can't you love a girl?'

73

she demanded, accusation in her tone, and he was taken aback.

'Goodbye, Dot.'

She waves a hand, then turns her face away, seeming overcome. He doesn't know why, just for a moment, he wants to tell her he has been widowed, that the wife she is jealous of died because she was concerned about chickens in a wooden box, that no arrogance or self-regard was smacked down by so absurd a death, only gentle modesty. In that same moment there is an urge that almost has its way: to connect past and present, to confess he could not love a girl because that is how he is, to throw in that he loves his child, a circumstance that still bewilders him. But nothing more is said.

Within minutes she'll be asleep, he guesses as he descends the narrow stairway. Thrown down on her bed, the smell of gin cloying on her breath, she'll drift through inebriated slumber and wake when her bed-sitting room is shadowy with twilight. A friend is what she needs, a friend from the present, not the past, some man to interest her in his hobbies, old coins or mill-wheels or choral singing. A man because she is a man's woman. A man to whom she might give what she has always wasted, her generous muddle of devotion and respect.

Beside Thaddeus in the car, Rosie's eyes are closed, her jaw propped on the edge of the passenger seat. He reaches out and runs the back of his fingers through her soft mane. She's company in a car, she likes being with him. 'Look!' Letitia exclaimed the day she brought her back, and he thought to himself this flea-infested, mangy animal will be a nuisance and an expense. Better to have left the creature to find her own way out of her misery, he wanted to say, but instead said nothing.

With only a line of pylons breaking his horizon, he drives as slowly as he always does. He bought his snub-nosed Saab for a few hundred pounds when the big end went in the grey van Mrs Ferry remembers. 'That jalopy'll go on for ever,' the man who sold it to him promised; eighty-seven thousand four hundred, the odometer registers now. Before the grey van there was his father's Aston Martin, which dated back to 1931, which of all his father's possessions his mother was most adamant they should not sell. 'We keep your father always. We see him in his things. We go to your father's church.' And every Sunday they did, walking there even when it rained. Twice a year Father Rzadiewicz drove her to Mass and afterwards played cards with her in the conservatory or the drawing-room she'd allowed to become tawdry, the old priest wearing his black mittens even in summer. The Aston Martin gave up on the road one day and had to be towed away, the repair that was necessary too expensive even to contemplate.

He was not able to love the bursar's daughter when he was still fifteen, although above all else he wanted to. He tried to say he did on all their walks, and in the trunk loft, his blazer flung down on dusty floorboards, sunlight from a roof window warming her expectant face, her brown hair soft in his fingers. 'Why *can't* you love a girl?' So very crossly that was demanded in Room Twenty, and elsewhere also. Disappointed in the end, would Letitia, too, have protested that passion wasn't enough in return for so much more?

Held up behind a lorry loaded with steel girders, an impatient sports car flashes its headlights. The lorry driver takes no notice, neither hurrying nor drawing in, and the lights are flashed again. Thaddeus turns off the main road, into the lanes.

Approaching the gateless pillars at the entrance to his house, he glimpses for an instant a flash of something white and blue – a child, it seems like, hurrying on a little used right-of-way through the fields. Even in the distance there is a familiar look about the figure, but Thaddeus does not pause to wonder why that is.

★

The car arrives, and then he's there. She didn't know that he was out somewhere. All the time on her journey she imagined him in the sunshine in his garden, and she wonders now where he has been. It could not have been the grave, for she'd have seen the car parked as she passed. Has he gone from shelf to shelf in a supermarket, having to because he has no wife to do it for him now? The dog is with him in the garden, and when he walks back to the house the dog remains.

She edges the door in the wall open, distrustful of the dog, but it doesn't come. An hour passes, and then the woman dressed in black appears. She picks something that grows close to the ground, a bunch of greenery she goes away with. Soon after that the dog comes to the door and Pettie pushes it closed. She opens it gingerly; the dog just looks at her, wagging its tail. She takes a chance, patting its head, and then it bounds off.

Yesterday, twice, she put the receiver down immediately when it was that woman who answered. But an hour or so later his voice said, 'Hullo,' and when she walked away from the phone box she could feel such happiness as she never

76

knew before. On the street two women stared at her and she stared back and laughed, wanting to tell them, wanting to say his name to them.

Trees protect her from the windows, a leafy barrier through which, after another wait, she watches the gaunt man light up a cigarette, far away in the yard. She noticed the green door in the arch of the high brick wall when he allowed her and the other girls to walk in the garden while they were waiting for the interviews. The two who kept together didn't speak, one and then the other going off when her moment came to ring the doorbell. She being the last, she waited longest and, passing the door in the wall for the second time, she opened it and saw leading from it the path through the fields.

The green paint has blistered and faded on the door. There is an iron casing within the archway that spreads two hinges in a pattern like the outline of a leaf on to the door itself. He has opened and closed this door. How many times? The metal latch is strong, moves easily, its tongue shaped for the thumb that operates it. How often has he touched it? How often does he still? She bends down to caress it with her lips. Her eyes are closed, a cheek pressed hard against the worn green paint.

Dusk comes, the last of the light pale in the sky. Reluctantly Pettie goes away, lingering to look back at the tall chimneys of the house, their brick arranged in decoration that can't be distinguished now, darkly silhouetted against the sky. On either side of the way through the fields she picks flowers she doesn't know the names of, and picks more from the verges of the lane. In the graveyard she finds a jam-pot on a neglected grave and fills it with water from a tap by the side of the church. Her flowers are colourful in the gloom, beside the withering blooms on the mound of fresh clay. She leaves them there for him to find, to comfort him in his grieving.

5

'Well, good days, bad days,' the nurse at St Bee's reports on the telephone, no tiredness in her tone, no hint of the tedium of having again to say what she has said so often before. There is a cheerfulness even, and Mrs Iveson recalls the slapdash features of the woman's face in which, as if to establish some kind of order, eyebrows are plucked and lips given a well-defined outline. She recalls the starched white uniform, the rinsed hair beneath the starched white cap, the watch pinned to a flattened bosom. When it was agreed that she should move to Quincunx House she rang St Bee's and explained to this same nurse about the change there was to be in her life and what had brought it about. 'Oh, my God!' the woman exclaimed then, her shock faltering into distress, sympathy offered when she recovered.

'You're settling in, Mrs Iveson?' she says now, three weeks after the arrangement was agreed, a fortnight after Thaddeus's rendezvous with Mrs Ferry.

'Later today.' A telephone number is given, repeated in St Bee's.

'It's marvellous of you, Mrs Iveson. It's simply marvellous.'

'Not really.'

'Indeed it is. Not that I don't envy you, an infant that age. Day to day, there's something new.'

'I suppose there is.'

It isn't true, but of course it doesn't matter. Chat there

has to be. Well, at least she has her grandchild, they would have commented at St Bee's when news of the death was earlier passed on. 'And to think he doesn't know!' would have been said, as so often it must be in this home. Georgina was called after him, he being a George, but he doesn't know that either.

'A joy at that age, I always say, not that it takes an iota away from the gesture you're making, Mrs Iveson. We're all full of admiration, we really are.'

She isn't young, they would have said; it's not as though she's young. Moving right in like that, not faltering or going to pieces, turning her back on what she knows, not that change isn't the best tonic when there's been what there has been. And of course it's natural, a daughter's baby.

'Never hesitate to call us up, dear. Don't ever think it's a nuisance, ringing up. In circumstances like this, I always say it's good to talk.'

'Yes.'

'Well, I have the details, dear. Thanks ever so.'

Both receivers are replaced in the same moment. Who says lightning doesn't strike twice? would have been said in St Bee's over cups of tea, the subject kept alive to ease the monotony of the day. No more'n a vegetable in tweeds, and now all this, the kiddy needing a mother's hand, fortunate the father's in agreement, unusual that.

I can't say I'm not nervous about this upheaval, Mrs Iveson last night finished a letter to her longtime friend in Sussex, *and perhaps this is not at all what Letitia would want. Well, if it doesn't work it doesn't. We can only try.*

She has let her flat to people called Redinger from Oregon, who say they like a good address. She chose them

80

because something about their manner suggested to her that they would be careful tenants. Their tenancy is for four months only, since that is the period of their stay in England; and when it finishes the agency will come up with other people, whom she can also personally vet if she wishes to continue to let the flat. She could less inconveniently have left it empty, visiting it herself from time to time to see that all was well. But the advice she has received is that empty property, these days, attracts burglary: the Redingers and any successors they may have would be caretakers as much as tenants. With that in mind, and against the wishes of the agency she employed, she has asked for only a modest rent.

Often during the days that passed while all this was so swiftly arranged, Mrs Iveson has experienced the doubts she expressed in her letter to her friend, but on each occasion has successfully wrangled with her misgivings. Within the tenancy agreement there is also a clause, specifically at the Redingers' request, that allows one month's notice on either side, should there be a change of circumstances. This is a comfort.

It is particularly so when Mrs Iveson looks through what remains in cupboards and drawers on the morning of her departure, as she unlocks and locks again the built-in wardrobe that contains the clothes she isn't taking with her. Everything is in order in the kitchen, the refrigerator empty, the electric kettle unplugged. The News comes unobtrusively from her Roberts radio, the sound turned down. Earthquakes in Russia, riots in Hong Kong, a body on a river path in Wales, carnage in Croatia. And five hundred pounds to be paid as compensation to a canary breeder who declares himself devastated after a single measure of seed swelled to ten times its bulk in his prize bird's stomach, destroying all chance of success at the Culross and Kincardine Cage-birds Festival.

'You've never known unhappiness, darling,' her own voice echoes, sounding harsh although she did not intend it to. In marriage she had not known unhappiness herself, and simply feared for her daughter in uncharted territory. That on an April afternoon there should have been an encounter on a train was a chance as cruel as life uselessly passing in a twilight room. You can't help loving someone, Letitia said, returning at her usual time from the music library less than two months later, not taking her coat off yet or putting down her handbag. And that was that.

Standing on a chair, Mrs Iveson reads the electric meter. Kneeling down, she reads the gas one. She notes both figures and leaves the piece of paper on the kitchen table, asking the Redingers to check them. On the radio a programme about people who collect things begins, a woman in Pontefract with an assortment of dental plates, a man with light switches, another with beer-bottle tops. She turns the voices off, realizing that she should have done so before reading the meters but deciding that a minute of the radio won't make much difference to the figure she has recorded.

She closes her kitchen door and sits down to wait by the window of her sitting-room. She gazes into the street below, where a smartly dressed tart is exercising her Pekinese. Not long ago she was taken for such a woman herself as she let herself in at the downstairs door. A man with a moustache in a teddybear coat raised his hat. 'Colette?' he smiled. 'I phoned.' This trade, in daytime, is a new thing in the neighbourhood.

The woman and the dog pass round the corner and then Thaddeus's car appears, his old blue car to which apparently he is attached. Letitia found that touching, as she did his attachment to his house and to his garden. A sentimental man, she said. The worst that could happen next was that unhappiness would come. Beyond imagination was what actually occurred.

The car is parked. Returning quickly, the woman with the Pekinese smiles. Thaddeus shakes his head. 'Oh, don't be silly,' Mrs Iveson vexedly upbraids herself. She blows her nose and crosses from the window to a looking-glass. She tidies her hair again and then is ready.

★

'Small mercies,' Maidment commented when it was decided that a nanny was not to be added to the household, and Zenobia unhesitatingly agreed. A sense of satisfaction – almost of celebration – has since prevailed.

For, old or young, such women have been a bane. Nanny Tub, remembered without pleasure in a house in Somerset, belonged to a regime that lingered from the past, an imperious termagant, disdainful and cantankerous as of right. Her replacement, when finally a replacement was considered necessary, complained that she'd been given catfood in a shepherd's pie. Another wouldn't touch meat in any form and had to have Oriental vegetable dishes prepared for her. A third took garlic in quantity for her health, its odour trailing behind her from room to room.

'We have to see, of course,' Maidment concludes, caution in his tone, 'how madam deploys herself.'

A racing paper, folded in two, lies between the couple on the scrubbed-oak surface of a table that is as strong as a butcher's block and as steady. It is all that remains of the kitchen as once it was: the black-leaded double range has gone, as have the ham hooks from the ceiling, the row of bells, the stone flags from the floor. It is a modern kitchen now. Working surfaces are pale moulded laminate, wall cupboards finished to match; deep-freeze and refrigerator, cooking hob and oven, dishwasher, tumble-drier and washing-machine are unified through shape and colour and design of detail. But the oak table still retains its slab of white marble set in the timber at one end, for many generations an aid to bread- and pastry-making.

'I foresee no troubled waters.' Zenobia rises from the table as she speaks, gathering up the cups from which mid-morning tea has been drunk, the brown kitchen teapot, jug, sugar bowl, and a plate with only the crumbs of a cake left on it. She stacks these dishes on a tray and carries the tray to a draining-board, where she separates them: milk and sugar kept to one side, the teapot rinsed beneath a running tap, everything else placed in a washing-up basin in the sink.

'Death is a trouble in itself,' Maidment remarks, which is a repetition voiced regularly since the tragedy, for when Maidment discovers a phrase he considers apt he is generous in his use of it. 'The good go quietly from us,' he quoted on the day of the funeral, the observation overheard in another house on a similar occasion.

'Life must go on,' Zenobia retorts through the rattle of dishes.

'I grant you that, dear. It's not grief's function to obstruct it.'

Shocked and sympathetic, the letters coming to the house have been read by Maidment, the daily stack of answers taken by him from the table in the hall to the postbox. 'I cannot help myself,' Zenobia apologized often during that time, weeping as she did her work. The will that was read left the couple a nest-egg substantial enough to allow eventual retirement without restriction. On that score, too, Zenobia's tears have been shed.

'I'm heating your milk, dear,' she addresses the baby, in her care this morning, while Mrs Iveson is fetched.

Sleepily occupying the pram that is her blue-and-white and most familiar world, incapable as yet of articulating more than private sounds, Georgina does not respond.

'Never a hope they'll get on,' Maidment pursues his reasoning, 'and of course were never meant to.'

'They've put our young friend here before their differences. You can't but admire that. There's been a side brought out in both of them.'

'I wouldn't go a bundle on admiration. I wouldn't put money on a side brought out.' Maidment draws in air, his lean nostrils tight for a moment in a way that is particular to him. He releases them while glancing at a line of print, noting that It's the Business, K. Bray up, is favoured if the going doesn't turn heavy, which is unlikely. Major Mack gives Rolling Cloud, P. J. Murphy's Guaranteed Good 'Un is Politically Correct. He favours The Rib himself.

'One minute and it'll be ready, dear.' Zenobia smiles with this annunciation, hoping that Mrs Iveson's advent will not deprive her entirely of the baby's company. She tests the milk and returns it to the bottle-heater, considering it not yet warm enough. The survivors share the burden of a child: that's what there is; the rest is wait and see. She does not press her conjecture of a moment ago, but deliberates instead.

He has his ways, he has his right to an opinion. Servitude has made him what he is and has — though differently — made her. All that, Zenobia accepts, and expects no more of their calling. Childless themselves — as so often and so naturally their predecessors in this kitchen have been — they are a couple who hang on in whatever households they can find. They are out of their time, which was a time when servitude had a place reserved for it, part of what there was. Their lives are cramped as much by this as by the exigencies of domestic duty, yet on neither count do they complain. They have chosen this; they have sensed the stirrings of vocation in serving the remnants of nobility or the newly rich. They have found a place in the great houses that are now the property of popular entertainers, that are now hotels and schools and residential business centres. They have visited on their Sundays off places of local interest in the many counties of their employment, this in particular being Zenobia's relaxation: Lydford Gorge and Mount Grace Priory, cathedrals and gardens, the narrowest street, the oldest tower clock. As they are presently settled so they hope they may remain, not moving on until age gets the better of them.

'And it may not,' Zenobia answers her own reflection, testing the temperature of the milk, squirting a drop on to her wrist. 'We trust in Providence.'

In The Rib more like, Maidment's thought is: O'Brien the trainer, The Rib will take some beating. Maidment has never been on a racecourse: what he knows, all he experiences of the turf, is at second-hand, but second-hand is enough. Epsom and Newmarket, the Gold Cup, the Guineas, the sticks, the flat: it is enough that they are there, that sports pages and television bring them to him. Rising from his chair, folding the newspaper away, he softly hums a melody he danced to as a boy, and prepares to go about his morning tasks, vacuuming and airing and dusting, setting things to rights. He tolerates old clocks and narrow streets, he does his best in gardens and in stately rooms that do not interest him. Other people's lives, how they are lived and what they are, offer what the vagaries of the turf do: mystery and the pleasure of speculation.

Zenobia hears the humming of her husband's tune continue in the kitchen passage and abruptly cease when he passes through the door to the hall. As he is unmoved by what she most enjoys, so she is not drawn to the excitements of the racetrack; and mystery for her is the mystery of the Trinity. Every night and morning she prays on her knees by her bedside; on Sundays her husband waits in their small red Subaru with the *News of the World*, while she attends whatever church they pass on their way to a place of interest. Disagreement between them no longer becomes argument, resentment does not thrive. Give-and-take patterns the Maidments' middle age; they go their ways and yet remain together.

'Oh, it is better so,' Zenobia comments, offering the opinion to her employer's child.

★

In the small room that opens out of the bedroom in which Thaddeus Davenant was born are the personal possessions he has kept by him, and photographs and papers. For the five years of his sojourn in this house Maidment has repeatedly examined them, expertly poking about in drawers and in the pigeon-holes of a writing desk, anywhere that is unsecured. Box-files are marked *Insurance, Receipts, Bank Statements, Accounts*. In a flat tin that once contained mint sweets there are keys that have never been thrown away, old fountain-pens, old watches, a yo-yo, an empty notebook, cufflinks separated from their match, tie-pins, dice, marbles. A shallow drawer is full of half-used seed packets. A silver hip-flask bears the initials *P. de S. D.*, and at the wheel of a sports car is a genial man whom Maidment has long ago recognized as the initials' source. He it was who attempted to resurrect the family's past by manufac-turing soap instead of the tallow that for generations had made its fortune, travelling the countries of Europe in search of orders. Pasted into an album now, he's there among trams and motor-cars in Vienna, and again in Amsterdam. He skates with a tall, beautiful girl on a frozen lake, is with her among the wild flowers of a hillside. Maidment knows her well: Hitler's war came, Eva Paczkowska was brought from Poland to England in the nick of time. Still beautiful, she stands smiling by the summer-house. Still beautiful, she's on the front-door steps, holding a child by the hand. But beside her the genial man she married is cadaverous now.

Maidment has searched but has never found snapshots of that child growing up. The camera seemed to have been put away. Only among the gowned ranks of schoolboys, framed on the room's dark wallpaper, is there a face he recognizes, reticent and private at that time.

Some tidying has taken place, he notices this morning. The wastepaper basket is full, papers that have accumulated since the death are no longer in a bunch beneath the bronze horseman on the windowsill. Cheque-book stubs indicate payments made that were not possible a week or so ago, before a simple probate was completed. Correspondence from solicitors has been relegated to a relevant file, letters of condolence ticked when they've been answered. The hiatus is over, the debris of death disposed of. The woman who asked for money has been visited, faith kept with a wife's last wish.

On the landing Maidment arranges towels and sheets in the hot cupboard, placing those not yet aired closer to the cistern. In the bedroom that is to be Mrs Iveson's he raises a window sash in order to expel a wasp, satisfies himself that the bulbs of the bedside lamps do not need to be replaced, extracts from the welcoming flowers a sweet-pea whose stem has failed to reach the water in the vase. 'The Rib, four thirty,' he keeps his voice low to instruct on the landing telephone. Palm cupped around the mouthpiece, he gives the racecourse details and makes his wager.

Outside, a car door bangs, there's Rosie's bark. Not hurrying, for Maidment never does, he makes his way downstairs, to carry up Mrs Iveson's suitcases.

★

The canal doesn't have any barges on it and only a sludge where there should be water. She discovered the towpath that runs by it the night she stayed late at the door in the wall and there wasn't a bus to the railway station. No one is about when she passes the broken petrol pump and the shop and the public house.

Seven times in all she has phoned in the weeks that have passed, five times replaced the receiver when it wasn't his voice. Twice she has put down flowers for him to find, but this afternoon she hurries by the graveyard, not going in to see if he has put fresh flowers down himself. This afternoon she's anxious to get to the door quickly.

She opens it cautiously, an inch or two, when she arrives, even though she has made friends with the dog. She can hear a movement in the undergrowth, not far from where she is. In a moment, paws scratch and the dog's nose is pressed through the crack. She can see its tail wagging and she reaches in and pats its head. It goes away then, as it did the other time.

'They called it the October house,' she hears after another long wait, his voice reaching her easily.

Sixteen-sided, the summer-house was built to catch the autumn sun, he is telling the old grandmother, who's dressed all in white. It was positioned with that in mind, he says, its windows angled for that purpose. The dog is with them, panting in the warmth.

'Well, that's most interesting,' the grandmother says, and Pettie can tell that this is what she has been dreading, that this old woman has come to take her place.

'The Victorians experimented more than people know.'

Some of what is said next is lost, but then they're nearer and he's talking about the trees, pointing at them. He refers to the grass of the lawns, saying he remembers a time when it was two feet high. Nettles grew through the heather-beds on the slopes, he says, and thistles in the rose-beds. The grandmother says something about a diary that went on and on, year after year, and he says oh yes, Amelia Davenant's journal, before his time.

'Letitia talked about it,' she says.

'Letitia liked it.'

It seems it's history now, this diary, written during some

woman's sleepless nights, yonks ago – entries about a chimney being swept and milk going sour and marmalade made, an Indian selling carpets at the door. A punnet of raspberries, picked and left down somewhere, could not be found. A cousin got engaged. The well didn't fill, a duchess was murdered in some foreign place. He's making conversation with all that; doing his best, you can tell from his voice. He doesn't want what has happened. He doesn't want this old woman in his house.

'At parties they used to dance outside. Waltzes lit from the downstairs windows and the front door. Music in the hall.'

'Yes. Letitia said.'

Some gardener or other came back from the trenches in a shocking state. 'He showed his wound to the children. Here, among his vegetable-beds. Among them was my father.'

Hinchley the gardener was called. His scar stretched from wrist to elbow because while an enemy soldier was inflicting it he was shot and fell forward, bringing this Hinchley to the ground with the bayonet trapped in his arm. After he'd shown the children his wound Hinchley always had a smoke apparently, a small, charred pipe for which he pared tobacco from a plug.

'Stories hang about old family houses like ghosts.' It was his mother who told him all that about the gardener; his father didn't tell stories much.

'Letitia kept a diary when she was little,' the grandmother gets her say in.

'Yes, I know.'

'It's interesting about the summer-house.'

You can tell she isn't interested in the least, even though she has said she is twice. She has wangled her way into the house, pulling the wool over his eyes with her talk. He was referring to that other diary and she has to bring Letitia into it, harping on the name when he's trying to forget it in his grieving.

She's on about a shoe now, a heel coming off when Letitia was little and Letitia not minding when she had to walk in her bare feet on a street. There's something about how Letitia went in for music, how she always had music going apparently, how she couldn't be without it. He makes some comment on that, but his voice is too low to carry.

'Well, I must go and see if my charge has woken up,' the old woman says.

Dismally, Pettie watches while he pats the dog's big brown head, the way he's always doing. A blackened tennis-ball falls by his feet, a paw prods his trousers. There's foam on the dog's tongue and when the ball is thrown it's carried back again and dropped at his feet.

'Thaddeus.' She says his name, louder than a whisper. Each day going by and the old woman still not here, she thought there was a chance. Just by looking at the old woman you can see it: anything goes wrong she'll be all over the place.

The ball is pushed against his shoe when he takes no notice. The dog's fond of him, standing back and barking now. Letitia'd never want it, an inadequate tending Georgina Belle. Grandmother or not, well longer than thirty years it would be since she tended a baby.

She says his name again. She wants to push the door wide open and go to him. She wants to tell him she knows he's hurting, to tell him she put the flowers there. She wants to tell him what Letitia would, that the baby isn't properly minded, that the baby isn't safe.

She watches while he smiles down at the dog. He throws the ball again, skittering it over the grass, and her longing is more than she can bear. She closes her eyes and his voice whispers between his caresses, saying he knows too well the old woman shouldn't be here. His fingertips are light on her skin, and on her lips when he whispers that it is their secret, that they have always had a secret, since the first day she phoned him up, that everything in the end will be all right. His arms hold her to him. He whispers that a thing like this can happen. He calls her his princess.

6

'You read that?' the red-haired proprietor of the Soft Rock Café asks, jerking a thumb at the newspaper open beside him. 'They got that car-tyre guy.' A car-tyre vandal, he says, eighteen hours' community service. A pound thirty-eight, he says, returning his vast metal teapot to the electric ring on which he keeps it hot. 'There you go,' he says.

Albert carries a glass mug of tea and one of coffee to a table and returns to the counter for the doughnuts. He puts a saucer over Pettie's coffee because she hasn't arrived yet. He didn't order her coffee, the man just set his machine going and put her doughnut in the microwave, maybe thinking she was outside on the street. Albert doesn't drink coffee himself, having read in a newspaper that it doesn't do you any good.

'What I'd do for vandals,' the red-haired man calls across the café, empty of customers except for Albert and the dumb man in the window, 'is bring the stocks back. Coat over the head's the first thing any villain wants. Know what I mean, Albert?'

Albert says he does, and hears about a young bloke beaten to a pulp when he wouldn't give two other blokes a bag of crisps. 'I'd have the cat o' nine tails back, Albert. Electrically operated, no call for anyone to demean their-selves working the cat this day and age. Know what I mean?'

Albert again says he does. Pettie doesn't like the red-haired man. He called her pert once; he said she'd fit into a thimble. Pettie complained that that was familiar, and Albert worries that something similar may have again offended her, that she may have come in on her own and taken exception, that because of it she won't come this morning. In Mrs Biddle's house she comes and goes when he's asleep, or at night when he's at work; half the time he doesn't know if she's there or not.

'You see Pettie around?' he asks the man, going back to the counter to do so.

'She ain't here yet, Albert.'

'She been in though?'

The man says no, not earlier, not yesterday, not the day before. He'd set the stocks up outside Burger Kings and Kentuckys, outside pin-ball joints, and toilets, in car parks – wherever people go by he'd have them. 'Settle their hash for them, languishing in the rain.'

When she arrives she starts the music. She lifts the glass saucer from her coffee. Ignoring the raspberry dough-nut that has been heated up for her, she lights a cigarette. She's wearing a different T-shirt, yellow with music on it.

'You OK, Pettie?'

She doesn't answer. She doesn't nod or shake her head.

'You got work then?'

'I feel for him, Albert.'

Albert looks away. He stares at the matador in one of the posters, then at the bull, head bent, horns ready to attack.

'I've been going out there,' Pettie says.

'The man with the baby, Pettie?'

'All the time I feel for him.'

Albert shifts his glance, allowing it to fall for a moment on the excitement that brightens his friend's features, her eyes lit with it behind her glasses. Distressed, he surveys the similar bull and matador of the poster on the opposite wall, then asks:

'You going to eat your doughnut today, Pettie?'

She shakes her head. She eases the wrapping from her cigarette packet and begins to make a butterfly of it. Albert watches her fingers twisting the transparent film. He asked her once who taught her how to make the butterflies, but she said she taught herself.

'He's old, Pettie. You said.'

'Forties. Why'd it matter?'

Her cigarette smoulders in the table's discoloured ash-tray, a thread of smoke floating lazily from it. The man in Ikon Floor Coverings was older too, fifty or so, Albert guessed. A tired face, she said. Albert remembers that although he never met, or even saw, the man. 'It could be he's gone off sick,' she said at this very table, before she discovered the man had moved on to another store.

'Every day I go out there.'

She tells about the difficult journey, the trains that are few and far between. Twice she'd had to thumb a lift on a lorry. The bus from the station goes round the long way and an hour it can be, waiting for it. You get there quicker if you walk by the drained canal. You turn away from the towpath when the spire of the church appears; you come out by the shop.

'You shouldn't go thumbing lifts, Pettie.'

'You have to, morning time.'

The lorries go down Romford Way, out beyond the Morning Star. If you get there early they'll stop. She wouldn't take a lift in a car.

'That man going to give you the job out there after all then?'

'As old as Mrs Biddle, the grandmother is. No more'n a laugh, Mrs Biddle minding a baby. The grandmother's got herself in there like she said she would.'

'Best left if there isn't work there, Pettie.'

'Left? How could you leave it?'

'Won't do you no good, Pettie. That place.'

She reaches for her cigarette, knocking off the ash that has accumulated at the tip. You're nearly at the gateless pillars when you take the path through the field, she says, the fir trees on your right at first. Every time the dog comes back to the house in the car it gives a bark, she says. First thing when it gets out, then again if the car comes back and it's not in it. Other times it don't bark at all.

'You take care with a dog, Pettie.'

'D'you understand what I'm saying to you, Albert?'

'You get a bite off a dog, you're in trouble. A woman got a bite off a dog that came over the wall –'

'I'm talking about something else.'

Albert nods. He knew she was, he says; it's just that any dog can be vicious. He read about the woman in the paper, stitches in her neck. He rubs the surface of the table with a finger, drawing a shape that isn't visible on it. He went in to ask at the Marmite factory, he says. He went to ask if there was anything for a girl, only they didn't have any-thing at present. He made enquiries in the KP, in the dairy yard, down the Underground. He heard they were looking for machinists up Chadwell way, but when he went in they said they weren't.

'Yeah,' she says.

'You eat your doughnut, Pettie.'

She picks her mug up and goes to get more coffee. Albert watches her, her thin legs beneath the denim skirt, her high heels clonking on the tiled floor. When first they ran away, when they were in the seed place, she said what she wanted was to get work in a store. Someone had left two car seats in a glasshouse and put corrugated up where the glass had gone. Stone was still on pallets around a rusting weighing-machine at one end, paving stones, quarry stones. Spreading out rolls of plant-sacking to lie down on, and fixing up shelving they found to keep the rain out where more glass had been broken, they used to talk about the work they'd try for when they had somewhere better to live. Pettie always said a store.

'You try the stores again?' he asks when she comes back. 'You been round them at all?'

She doesn't answer, stirring her coffee. He heard the red-haired man saying the T-shirt suited her, but she didn't bother with that either. She tastes her coffee and breaks a bit off her doughnut, the fat on it no longer glistening because it's cold. She says she gave up the stores yonks ago. Same's she gave up the idea of getting office skills. Same's she gave up trying to get work at the swimming-baths.

'If there's a vacancy at the Marmite, you'd go for it, Pettie? The woman said keep in touch.'

Yeah, great, she says, but he knows she doesn't mean it. He tries for a distraction, drawing attention to Air India going over. Always at this time, he reminds Pettie, smiling at her, twenty to eleven. No way that's anything but Air India.

'Rosie the dog's called.'

His smile remains when he shakes his head. 'Won't do no good, Pettie.'

'I put flowers on the grave.' She wipes a smear of jam from around her lips. 'The grandmother's beyond it.'

'You still all right for the rent, Pettie?'

She doesn't answer, and he explains that Mrs Biddle won't be put upon. In case she has forgotten, he mentions that. He has known it before, he says, this state she's got into, having feelings for this man. It's the same thing happening all over again.

'It's not the same. It's like you're waiting for something and then it happens. It's like it's meant, Letitia gone, then the advertisement.'

'I know what you mean, Pettie.'

'You hear her voice, you know it's meant.'

'It's only you wouldn't want to lose the room.'

She doesn't look at him, she doesn't care. Despair comes as a hollowness in Albert's stomach, a cavity of dull, unfeeling pain. Within a week of losing her room she'll be up Wharfdale.

'The grandmother falls asleep,' she says. 'I seen her at it.'

★

The receiver is put down, and Pettie visualizes it on the table in the hall, where she noticed a telephone while she sat there waiting. Clearly she recalls the dark panelling in the hall, the half-open door of the dining-room, the sluggish tick of the clock.

'I'm sorry,' he says, coming back when she is beginning to

think that maybe he won't, that maybe he hasn't understood. 'I've asked, but no ring has been found.'

'I think maybe where I was sitting. On that settee. I think maybe it slipped under a cushion. A finger-ring,' she says.

Again the receiver is placed on the table's surface, more of a rustle than a thud, as if his hand is partly over the mouthpiece as he lays it there. There are his footsteps moving away, and then there are different, distant sounds. She puts another coin in the slot. She lights a cigarette. She couldn't stop smoking after she went back to the Floor Coverings place with the tie she had acquired, and the book about tennis stars because he'd said he liked to watch the tennis. 'Oh, Eric's gone,' they said, putting an end to what hadn't yet begun. She stood there looking at them and they asked her if she was all right. How could she search for him? she thought, and yet she trailed from store to store.

'No, nothing there, I'm afraid.'

His voice is as it was when first she heard it, when he gave her directions, on the telephone also. It's soft, just a little different from what it is when she hears it in the garden or as it was at the interview. But not a whisper; every word is clear. Again he says he's sorry.

'I've pulled the cushions out,' he says.

She wonders if settee is right. Couch she might have said, but it wasn't called that when she was there, and she remembers now that the grandmother said sofa. Finger-ring was Miss Rapp's word. 'Grey soapstone,' Miss Rapp said when someone asked. 'Mother's grey soapstone.' Just say a ring and it could be a curtain ring or something for an ear.

'No, sentimental only,' she says when he asks if it's valuable. She must have fiddled with it, nervous because of the interview, she says, because she wanted the position so. She must have slipped it up and down her finger. She only noticed afterwards, in the train.

'I didn't like to bother you before, sir. I didn't want to be a nuisance, a time like this for you. But then I thought that's silly.'

'It's no trouble at all.'

'I was the last girl that came on the Friday. I think you remarked I was the last.'

'If you could let me have a phone number or an address we'll let you know if your ring is found.'

There are twenty pence left, registered on the screen. She has another coin ready in case it's necessary, a fifty. She wonders if he's wearing his fawn shirt and light-coloured trousers, the brown leather shoes that could do with a shine. He doesn't wear a chain or anything, nothing on the wrist or at the neck.

'D'you think I could come out, Mr Davenant? Could I look on the driveway in case it slipped off there?'

He doesn't say anything and for a moment she thinks the money has run out, that they have been cut off. But the screen says 16p. Once he had other shoes on in the garden, canvas, light-coloured like his trousers.

'I'm afraid it's a little like a needle in a haystack.'

She can feel his concern, as she did when first she said she'd lost something. Thaddeus suits his voice as well as his appearance. It suits an older man. When you get used to it you realize he couldn't be called anything else.

'Maybe it's silver, or only silver-coloured. The gem's a soapstone. Grey.'

'Well, I'm sorry to say we haven't found it.'

'I'd have a look along the lane I walked on. All right to do that, Mr Davenant?'

'Of course it is. And if you do, please come back here and see for yourself.'

For a moment Pettie cannot speak. In the silence she hears his breathing and knows everything is different because he has said that. No two people could have more in common than a baby: Georgina Belle, and the long days of his bereavement becoming shorter, time the healer. In the silence she can feel the closeness again, like there was when he held his hand out, the moment their hands touched. Like when she looked at the photograph among the flowery paperweights, when he saw her looking and didn't have to say anything.

'I'll come,' she says, and asks him when she should.

★

'I never wanted her here.'

'It's only temporary, Mrs Biddle. Pettie's down on her luck, but that's just for the moment. Pettie'll walk in with news of a job and it'll be like it used to be.'

'She'll get up on her legs and go is what she'll do.'

Albert mentions the Dowlers. He explains that he has looked up Dowler Drains in the telephone directory, 21A Side Street. No way the Dowlers won't take Pettie back when he puts it to them.

'Pettie's got into a muddle, Mrs Biddle.'

'The time I woke up she was standing there with a camel in her hand.'

'Pettie was only looking at the camel, Mrs Biddle.'

'She could look at it on the mantelpiece, nothing stopping

her. She could stand there looking at it all day, only she never come in when I'm lying awake. Creeping about the place, that girl'd get you into an early grave. She was nicking that camel. She'd nick the whole display, give her a chance.'

'Soon's she hears no problem with the Dowlers she'll be OK.'

'You have a room, you pay for it.'

'It's only I'm worried what'll happen to her.' Albert mentions Bev gone missing and Marti Spinks and Ange up Wharfdale. He mentions Joey Ells.

'You told me about Joey Ells. We're talking about paying the rent.'

'If the chutes wasn't clogged, there'd have been water in that tank. Could've been she was lying there drowned.'

Propped up on her pillow, the backs of her hands cool at last after the day's heat, Mrs Biddle quotes thirty-six pounds as the sum due to her. It isn't much to pay for getting rid of a girl you didn't want to have near you in the first place, but she refrains from saying so.

'Joey Ells can't hardly walk ever since.'

'You told me, Albert. It lowers me to hear about Joey Ells. I'm low enough without hearing about Joey Ells all over the place.'

The hot weather brings out a testiness in Mrs Biddle. All day long, wafting in through her open windows, the comments of the pedestrians on the pavement outside have had to do with the unabating heat. A drought is spreading throughout the country, the television News has three times informed her. Even though it's gone eight and the evening cool has come, grown men go by in shorts.

'She can creep about somewhere else. You tell her that

from me, Albert. You tell her if she paid what's owing ten times over she's not coming back to that room. Par for the course, this is.'

'I'd call in at the Dowlers' tonight.'

'That girl ain't coming back here.'

He'll call in at the Dowlers' all the same, he says. His smile has gone; his eyes are dull. There isn't often any kind of disagreement between them. In a flat voice he asks:

'You got an appetite now the warmth's gone? You fancy pilchards?'

She says she would and he goes to open a tin, leaving the door open because she likes to hear him in the kitchen. Smells waft in and she likes that too. 'Make us a bit of toast?' she calls out, and he says he will.

Extraordinary, that he'd be mixed up with a girl who'd sweet-talk her way into a bed-ridden woman's house. All you have's your house, the view from the window, folk going by. You can't be expected to take in all and sundry. 'Lovely animals,' was what the girl said when she was caught with the camel.

'All right then, Albert?'

He calls back, saying he is. She tries the television, but all that happens is snow coming down. She turns it off and watches a woman across the street sweeping the pavement in front of her door. He's far from all right, with that girl affecting him, that Joey Ells coming up the way she always does. The last few weeks he's not been himself by a long chalk.

The woman across the street leans on her brush, talking to a gas man. A car turns into the terrace and West Indian people get out of it, a man laughing, a girl with a sleeping baby. She can smell the toast now. When he comes in with the meal she'll soothe him. They had to have the upset, but it's behind them now. She'll try to get it to him that they'll be like they used to be.

'Television's gone on the blink again,' she says when he comes back, not wanting to rush in with the other immediately. His arms are tense, carrying the tray in the careful way he has, clutching it tightly. When he pushes the door closed with his elbow she says that the upset's over and done with, that she had to put her foot down. She advises him to put the girl behind him, same's he should that Joey Ells. 'You forget them bad things, Albert. There's no one can look after me better'n you do. No one ever did.'

He places the tray on the bedclothes the way she likes him to do, not too far down, so that she doesn't have to sit up more.

'You having enough there, Albert? You make more toast if you want to.'

'No, I've enough.'

'You don't want to starve yourself. You take what you want.'

'I'm all right.'

'I like a pilchard, Albert.'

She brings in Bolton then, reminded by the fish. Tomkins Avenue, Number Seventeen, and Harvey Clegg put the breakfast herrings down the armchair. Nineteen forty-nine it would have been.

'A Mrs Frist that landlady was, thin little woman, sharp's a tooth. Couldn't stand her, Harvey couldn't, and the herrings was off. Stank the house out inside of a day and she knew, of course. She said she'd have the law on him.'

He wags his head; she can tell he's interested. He's interested in everything, he likes to hear. She takes a mouthful of tea, washing bits of pilchard from under her teeth, then settling the teeth back into place.

'He was always up to something, that Harvey Clegg. The time he brought the Widow Twanky into *Little Red Riding Hood* you'd have laughed your head off. "Next for shaving, the Widow Twanky!" he shouted out when Red Riding Hood'd just said what big eyes. Not a pick of sense it made, but they roared.'

His head is cocked to one side a bit, as it is when he listens for his planes, but all there is to hear is the distant traffic in Bride Street. He finishes his pilchards, always quick with his food. He turns the television on, then goes behind it.

'You getting a picture now?'

There's sexual intercourse, which is on constantly these days. Either that or people at death's door in a Casualty. Or it's the female who reads out letters and winks at you, some kind of tic she has.

'That OK now, Mrs Biddle?'

She changes the channel, pressing the numbers on the remote control. Blood spatters a wall and drips over a vase of flowers. A boot is kicking the stomach out of a body on the ground.

He goes on fiddling, then comes round to look himself, and she says that's OK now, they can turn it off. He does so and the picture disappears, taking with it another thump of the boot, and frenzied music that is beginning to give her a headache. On the street outside an old man goes by, unkempt and bleary-eyed in the gathering dusk.

'She took advantage, Albert.'

He piles his own dishes on to her tray and waits for hers. One morning he didn't come in and she thought he was dead. Out on the streets in the night hours, someone like him could easily be set on because he's the way he is, because he's different.

'I'll make a jelly,' he says. 'Greengage. For tomorrow.'

The door closes behind him and then she hears him beginning to wash up. After that he'll go and have his evening rest. They told him down the platforms he must have his sleeps and he always does. She listens to the clatter of the dishes, then drops off for a moment, waking to hear his footsteps in the room above her. The day she managed the stairs when he was resting, his sleeping face was like an angel's, the empty eyes closed over, lips parted a little. Everything in the room was tidy around him, the little decorations on the walls. Sometimes all she wishes for before she goes is to have his worries taken from him, to know he'll be all right when she isn't there to think about him. When she can't move at all, which won't be long now, she wouldn't mind it if he washed her. He could bring the basin in and lift her nightdress off. She'd lie there with something else private between them, not anyone else's business, like the upset over the girl isn't.

7

Mahonia shoots shrivel, the elaeagnus is arrested. The climbing hydrangea droops, the leaves of the smoke shrubs have lost their sheen. Thaddeus's spinach goes to seed, the potatoes he digs are small. The drought is worse than the drought of 1976; the worst, so people interested in such matters say, for two hundred years. In the fields the sheep are fed hay, cattle are parched when streams dry up.

But the apple trees in Thaddeus's garden are laden, the pear trees and the plum orchard. Gooseberries and redcurrants ripen before their time. Cosmos has grown high, its misty foliage heavy with purple flowers, and pink and mauve and white. Butterflies flap silently through the buddleia.

Beneath the catalpa tree, with her grandchild on a tartan rug beside her deckchair, Mrs Iveson reads. Casting shadows on the pages of her book, lacy white panicles hang among the vast leaves, their scent delicate in the heat. *On a cold grey morning in late December Mr Charles set forth as usual, his letters stamped and sealed. Miss Amble greeted him, Mrs Mace a moment later. To both he raised his hat.* The plump housemaid did it, Mrs Iveson's thought is, before *The Mystery of the Milestone* slips from her fingers.

★

When you had collected seven transfers from seven tins of cocoa you sent away the seven pictures they made and received in return a statuette of Snow White. With a crust of bread clamped between her teeth, skinning and chopping two onions, Zenobia remembers that. She washes carrots and parsnips beneath a running tap, then trims the fat from a tenderloin of pork. Duplicates wouldn't do. She had Sneezy twice and Happy four times and still had to go on collecting. Her father said you'd maybe drink forty gallons of cocoa to get it right. He declared the whole thing a disgrace, on a par with chain letters and brush salesmen at the door.

'She has settled in,' she hears, as from a distance, her husband admit. 'I have to say you were right.'

Removing the bread from her mouth, she is startled: that does not come easily from him. He was certain there would be fireworks, unease at the very least. In spite of a loss two days ago at Ascot, he has given in gracefully; and Zenobia knows better than to gloat.

'It's early days yet, of course,' she acknowledges, since that seems only fair.

'She has come to accept what must be accepted.'

Maidment has inspected the newcomer's correspondence. Letters are often left not yet completed on her dressing-table, all to her friend in Sussex, whose replies later tie up loose ends. At the kitchen table, replacing one of the lugs that hold the strap of his wristwatch, he agrees that the blood tie of the child has made the difference.

'As you said yourself,' he graciously repeats. His beaky features are bent close to his task, the spigot in the spring of the metal lug repeatedly slipping as he attempts to prise it home with the blade of a knife. He experiences neither frustration nor impatience. Sooner or later, he knows he will succeed. Mr Nice Guy he should have gone for, but that is water under the bridge.

'Whoever's that?' Zenobia exclaims when the jangle of the hall-door bell sounds.

Achieving success before this dies away, Maidment returns his watch to his wrist and goes to answer the summons.

★

Kneeling on a plastic fertilizer sack, scattering the seeds of his winter parsley in a shady corner, Thaddeus wonders if in these conditions they'll germinate. Carefully, he waters, then places a sheet of glass on the four lengths of wood he has used to construct a square around what he has sown. Weeks will pass before the first green specks arrive, for if they do so at all they'll come slowly, the dendritic formation following at that same slow pace.

The summer has settled into a pattern of its own. Its days go ordinarily by in a season that belongs to circumstance, time dawdling, tranquillity a balm. The constitution of the household, which prospectively he feared, seems right to Thaddeus now: faith kept with unexpressed wishes, as it was with a last request.

'There's that girl, sir,' Maidment interrupts his thoughts, calling out, still some yards away. 'The girl about her lost ring, sir.'

Thaddeus nods, remembering the girl, knowing what all this is about. Maidment knows too, having been asked to keep an eye out for a ring. It could have been hoovered up, he said at the time, but he believes that is most unlikely.

Thaddeus gathers together the tools he has used, folding the plastic sack as he moves towards his house. He leaves it, with fork and trowel, at the front steps, to take to the yard later.

'If you ask me,' Maidment remarks dismissively in the kitchen, 'that ring never came into the house.'

The girl is after compensation, he suggests. Some devious way of claiming compensation, which nowadays is very much the fashion. Mingy little thing, he says.

★

She watches him feel with his hand under the sofa, crouched and stretching, then on his knees. He shakes his head when he stands up. He pulls the cushions out. All this has been done already, he says, but it's better to be certain. No luck? he says when she has searched, herself.

When their hands touch on the sofa he gives no sign. She wonders if the scent of the perfume she put on is reaching him, Flowers of Egypt, that she came by when the saleswoman was maundering on about New Shade lip salve. She went back to EasiEyes for the smoky frames, and paid for having them changed, but she hasn't seen him noticing that the frames are different from the ones she wore before. If he remarked on them she had it in mind to make him smile by saying she once tried contacts but they were like having shop windows stuck in. 'I'm old enough to be your father,' he might have said if anything had happened, if they stood up together and found themselves close. Sorrowing gets to you, he might have said, saying also that he shouldn't have done that, that he got carried away. No, it's all right, she had it in mind to reassure him. She knew, she understood.

They go upstairs. He pulls the curtains away from a window, looking down at the stair-carpet, explaining that unfortunately it would have been hoovered. She runs her fingers beneath an edge of it and then beneath another edge. Grey, she says again, a single grey stone, her mother's, and adds that her mother settled in the outback of Australia.

'I'm sorry,' he says. 'But I rather think we're not going to find it.'

She stands beside him by the nursery door. The house feels empty, although she knows it isn't. It's quiet, as it was before, and again the way it seemed the first evening she pushed open the green door. An older sister brought her up, she says, and when he smiles, but doesn't ask about that, she adds that her older sister went off years ago.

'To Australia?'

'Oh, yes.'

'Look wherever you like in here.'

Her mother writes every week, she says. Every Tuesday, sometimes a Wednesday, there's a newsy letter. She'd like to travel, she says.

He smiles and nods. He pulls an armchair to one side in order to look under it. 'Nanny's armchair,' the old grand-mother said that day. She helps him push it back again.

'It's a lovely nursery, Mr Davenant.'

'Yes, I suppose it is.'

'You don't often see a picture done like that. On a floor.'

'No, I don't suppose you do.'

'Were you a child in this house too?'

'Well, yes, I was.'

'It's a lovely house. The garden's lovely.'

'Yes, it is.'

Pettie smiles, looking up at his face. There is a star, she can't remember who it is, with flecks of grey in his hair and those same pale eyes. She can see him clearly, in evening dress and nonchalant, leading a woman in a gown to a restaurant table, the waiter bowing and scraping, an orchestra.

'You remind me of someone, Mr Davenant.'

'Do I?'

She dared to say it because he's still unaware, nothing in his voice except the softness she feels caressed by. He does not know that everything is special as they stand here now. He does not know that comfort and consolation in his grieving can come from somewhere.

'A star,' she says.

'Star?'

'Who you remind me of.'

He shakes his head. She wants to tell him she can hear the music of an orchestra, the people in that restaurant moving on to the dance-floor. She wants a conversation to begin, to tell him that this is her kind of music, to ask him if he likes the smoky frames, if the scent of Egyptian flowers is reaching him, if perfume on a girl is what he likes. Five times in all he has said he's sorry, including on the phone. When first she was alone with him, when the grandmother was out of the room, she found herself trembling and for a moment had to grip the sofa cover. It was then she knew something was up and ever since she has been a different person, just thinking about him. She wants to say that. She wants to say that they have stood together in the firelight with glasses of sherry, that he has put his arms around her and held her to him. She wants to share it with him, but of course there can't be that.

'A lot of children,' she says, 'must have played on that picture. I can just see them.'

'Yes.'

'I love children.'

'I'm sorry we weren't able to offer you the position here.'

'I know you're sorry, Mr Davenant.'

'It is a difficult time for us. What we decided is best, I think.'

The knee that's nearer to him touches some part of his leg when she slightly moves. 'I would give you the world, Pettie,' her Sunday uncle used to whisper, the first to call her by that name. His loving little princess, he whispered, the only one there would ever be for him. It was Eric who said he was old enough to be her father, and then said he was busy now.

'I thought I'd got the job. When you was telling me the directions to get here I thought it was all right.'

'Oh, no, no.'

'It doesn't matter.'

She laughs, pretending it doesn't. It was silly of her to make that presumption. When she rang the doorbell that afternoon she kept thinking she was coming home at last, and that was silly too. She laughs again, telling him that, but he's as solemn as he was before.

'Well, I'm afraid we haven't found your ring.'

He has been standing back to let her pass through the doorway in front of him, but now he doesn't any more. He goes first and she follows on the landing, their moment shattered. Other doors are open that were closed when she was here before, a bedroom and then another bedroom.

'It doesn't matter about the ring.'

'You've had a journey for nothing.'

'No, not for nothing.'

He just walks on, not asking what that implies. She sees his ties, striped and dotted, on a closet rail. A dressing-table is between two bay windows, a trouser-press. Hairbrushes are by a looking-glass on a pedestal. Curtains and wall-paper are a match, huge flowers like roses. It is just a glimpse, then there are the staircase pictures – paintings of different people, men and women, a picture of the house long ago, farm workers drinking in a harvest field.

'Oh, that is nice.' She stops and he stops also. 'Everything is lovely here.'

She wants them to stand there for a moment longer, as they stood together in the nursery, but he goes on, one hand on the banister, his footsteps hardly making a sound. He would have worn every one of those ties, he would have knotted them and straightened them in that mirror. Every day, every morning and maybe again later, his brushes touch his hair. He folds away his clothes, he lies asleep in that room.

'I'm sorry about your wife,' she says, and wants to tell him that she has looked into the garden from the door in the wall, that she has come back and come back again, that she knows about the summer-house and about the garden-er's bayonet wound, that she knows his wife's name was Letitia, that she knows his wife loved music.

'Thank you.'

They are in the hall; the dog is waiting there. It sounds strange, thanking her because she's sorry. He keeps on moving, touching the dog's head as he passes, crossing the hall to the front door. She wants to say she wouldn't feel jealous of his wife, or be against her, that there is nothing like that.

'I cried on the lane, thinking about your wife.'

He looks away, nodding as he opens the front door. The dog comes up to her, knowing her, wagging its tail.

'I went into the graveyard.'

He frowns, just slightly, then he nods again, standing by the open door.

'You said that day it was an accident on the road.'

'My wife was knocked off her bicycle.'

'I thought she might have been in a car.'

'No.'

'I don't know why I thought that.'

'She had gone to fetch some pullets. She looked behind her for a moment, maybe because the box on her carrier felt unsteady. That's what the driver saw. There's a bend on the hill she was going down.'

'I don't think I know pullets.'

'Young hens.'

She has saddened him; she has made him more sombre than he was. She didn't mean to. She should smile, and take his fingers from the door edge and close the door again, pressing out the ugly sunlight. She should lean against it and be cheerful, telling him she has her own name for his baby: Georgina Belle.

'Would you mind if I just looked once again in that room?'

'Of course not.'

He doesn't come with her, which she hoped he would. From the windows she can see the old woman in her deckchair beneath the tree, the baby on the patterned rug. In the room the photograph is still there, among the glass paperweights. Petals have fallen from a vase of flowers. In all her life she has never hated anyone as much as she hates the old woman: suddenly, Pettie knows that. She stands in the centre of the room thinking it, not looking for anything, since there is nothing to look for.

'No luck?' he says in the hall.

'No.'

'I don't think you were in the conservatory that afternoon?'

He indicates it, to his left. Beyond a glass door, framed in white, rows of orange-coloured pots have different kinds of flowers in them, pink and yellow, shades of blue. Green foliage trails all over the slanted glass, two wicker chairs with cushions on them have a wicker table to match.

'That's a beautiful place, isn't it?'

'You didn't go in there, though, that day?'

'No, I wasn't in there.'

'If we had a number to contact you on we could let you know if your ring turns up.'

'I put flowers on the grave, Mr Davenant.'

'What?'

'I put flowers on your wife's grave.'

He doesn't speak for a moment. Again he frowns a little, which is understandable. He says:

'We came to a decision about a nanny. There isn't a vacancy for one any more.'

'You said.' She waits for a moment, sorting out the words in her head, getting them right. 'I was brought up by a grandmother, Mr Davenant. She never managed.'

'I thought –'

'That was before. My sister came before. My nan was never up to it is what I'm saying.'

'I'm sorry. I'm afraid I don't entirely follow this.'

'There were accidents, like. Any old woman'd get dozy. An old woman drops off in the sun. Anything like that.'

'There really isn't a vacancy –'

'It don't matter about the vacancy, Mr Davenant. I didn't come out about the vacancy. I didn't put the flowers on because I thought you'd change your mind. The flowers was different. The heatwave killed the others, they was a sorry sight.'

'If we find your ring –'

'It doesn't matter about the ring. The ring's the least of it.'

'Even so, if ever we should find it we'd want you to have it back.'

He has opened the door as wide as it will go now. Although he's tall there's a slightness about him, a delicacy about his hands and slender wrists, the top button of his shirt undone beneath the grey knot of his tie. A fine silver chain is what she'd like to give him, without a medallion, nothing flash.

'It's terrible, what happened,' she says.

'What's terrible?'

'Your wife.'

He looks away. He mentions the ring again and she says again that it doesn't matter. It could have dropped off in the garden, she says, but he doesn't suggest they should look for it there. In a minute, in less than a minute more likely, she'll have gone, passed out of his company, everything over.

When her tears begin to come she looks away herself, not wanting him to see. But he notices, as she should have known he would, being the kind that does.

'Look, I'm awfully sorry.'

He might offer her his handkerchief, as she saw once, in a film it probably was. When he doesn't she roots for a tissue, but doesn't find one. He says he'll keep an eye out in the garden.

'Unless you'd like to look yourself.'

She shakes her head. She wants to say that all the time she has been in his house she has longed to tell him there is no ring and never was, to begin at the beginning, the afternoon when they were first alone. She wants to go to him in the silence that has come, to reach out and put a hand on his arm.

'Just flowers growing wild,' she says instead, since he has not denied that it is terrible about his wife. 'I put them in a jam-pot.'

★

Inspector Ogle prowled about, not knowing where to begin. Sir Hector had been drinking heavily that night, of that there was not the slightest doubt. He had 'emptied a bottle' according to the landlord. There seemed little doubt that he'd been drunk when he was murdered, that he was only blearily aware of his assailant's purpose. Ogle pondered, his long face further lengthened in concentration . . .

Mrs Iveson ponders too. The plump housemaid has had a past, may even have been illegitimately born to Sir Hector Greystiff. There was a reference earlier that suggested that, she can't remember what.

The girl who lost her ring comes down the front-door steps and slowly crosses the tarmac. Something about her movements suggests that the ring has not been found. Mrs Iveson turns back a page of *The Mystery of the Milestone* and begins it again before glancing up. The girl on the tarmac looks towards her for a moment, stands still and stares, and then goes on.

★

Maidment keeps the hall door open for a while in an effort to expel the oppressive odour of Flowers of Egypt.

'High and low they went,' he comments crossly in the kitchen. 'I could have told them.'

'Precious to the girl, it probably is.'

'No ring was lost in this house.'

'You'd have noticed it, of course.'

'The song and dance, it could have been the Crown Jewels.'

With that, the visit passes without further interest into the couple's memory, and other matters are spoken of.

★

'She was hoping to come here,' Thaddeus says on the lawn beneath the catalpa tree, 'even though we said no.'

Briefly that is wondered about, bewilderment silencing what might be said. Then in the garden, too, interest in the visit recedes and finally dissipates, the visitor forgotten.

8

Cow parsley is high in the hedgerows, foxgloves decorate the verges. Joe Minching said he worked the farms once, moving from place to place, all over the country. Silage-making and harvesting, lifting potatoes.

She walks slowly, going nowhere. She doesn't know what the crops on either side of her are, barley or wheat or oats, undisturbed on a breezeless day. There are fields of peas, and new green plants sprouting in the dry earth. A tractor is working somewhere, a low hum reaching her over flat landscape that's varied only by what is grown.

'I feel for you,' she whispered, close to him when she'd said about putting the flowers in the jam-pot. 'I feel for you,' she said again. He gave a kind of shrug, and she knew he thought she meant because he had been left a widower.

The sun is hot on her head and the back of her neck, a white glare in her eyes. Lost in the network of lanes, she is deep in the countryside now. She picks peas and eats them, sitting in the shade at the edge of a field.

He went down on his hands and knees; with a poignancy that softens her distress, she remembers that too. He stood by that nursery door and a beam of sunlight slanted across the room and lit up his pale eyes. 'We'd supply the uniform, of course,' he said the first time, on the phone. She could be with him now as he had wanted her to be, as she would be if there hadn't been an old woman's interference. Over and over again he said he was sorry.

The disappointment fills you and then empties; nothing's left except what might have been, what should be still. 'Oh yes, my dear': just for her there was that murmur on a Sunday afternoon, special and only for her. 'Oh yes, my princess,' and no one ever heard. On the side of his cheek the birthmark was shaped like a crescent moon and once she touched it.

She slips peas from another pod, then throws them away. 'The day will come I'll give you anything you want.' He had to come near, his breath warm on her cheek. 'Everything I have, darling, when I take you away with me.' A pencil-sharpener that was a globe of the world it was the first time, a Minnie Mouse watch later on. 'I never mind,' she said, looking away while she did what he wanted her to do, not wanting to see but still not minding. He didn't take to any of the others because only she was affectionate, because she said all sorts of things to him, how she liked being with him, how she'd be awake and think about him. She didn't mind that he was corpulent, the word Miss Rapp used when she noticed him going by in the downstairs passage once. She didn't mind anything about him because he meant it when he called her his princess and said he was her lonely king. Because he lived alone that was, in a house he'd bring her to one day, a house that was warm and dim, with a long back garden, aubrietia in his rockery, and once he brought a sprig to show her what aubrietia was. 'Wife and kiddies,' Joe Minching contradicted, and she said no. 'Pull the other one,' Joe Minching said. 'Oh, definitely.' It wasn't true, she shook her head, but when she asked again it seemed she had misunderstood. If only it could be, was what there was now; of all things in the world he would choose it, he wanted only that. His treasure, his lovely princess.

You don't believe it won't be all right. You don't believe you'll go back to the flooring place and they'll say you frightened Eric off. You don't believe an old woman will get in the way with her venom. On the seaside outing the fishermen pulled in their boats, the shingle rasping on the wood, and when the last of them went by, ruddy-cheeked, in wading boots, he smiled and said that mackerel was what they caught. She walked on with him while the others played and he pointed up the cliffs to where he lived, lifting his arm and you could see his jersey needed a darn. She'd have done it for him. She'd have gone with him to his house.

Her feet are sore. She takes her shoes off. 'I'm sorry,' her Sunday uncle whispered when he told her that she could never see the aubrietia in his rockery, offering her instead another sprig. His wife was sharp-voiced when she phoned her up, screaming abuse. His wife said accusations like that should be reported, you couldn't throw filth around and get away with it. But nothing was reported. And nothing was when she asked Joe Minching where the house was and cut the woman's clothes with a razor-blade, when she poured away her powder and marked the television screen with her lipstick. She cut the sheets on her bed and on her children's beds, and dumped stuff in the dustbins, and smashed the light-bulbs in the rooms: nothing was said, there was no complaint. She knew there wouldn't be. Nothing happened except that he didn't come back to the Morning Star.

It's different now. The empty, pale blue sky, the green pea

stalks, and grass and clay: all that makes it different, like looking for the ring together did. When he said, No luck? he wanted her to be in luck, he wanted everything to be all right. He wanted her to tend his baby, to give it all her love: in the nursery you could tell he wanted that. His voice is as it always is; it has not left her, his face has not blurred.

When she reached up for the fisherman's hand it was only to be affectionate, and when the rictus began in his face she thought he was smiling back, but he wasn't. He couldn't go quickly on the shingle, his flopping fisherman's boots a drag, holding him for another instant to her. When he was far away she picked a stone up, and felt her bitterness like vomit in her stomach when she tried to damage his boat. Riff-raff was what the old woman would have said, is maybe saying it again. The other woman was snooty on the landing that afternoon, you could tell by the way she looked. It was only him that wasn't, and he never would be.

Pettie walks again, and rests again, and then the evening shadows come, and lengthen as she watches, the shapes of trees and stubble softening. Joe Minching walked coast to coast, he said, labouring at anything, killing rabbits, skinning squirrels, sleeping out. She'd have gone with him if he wanted it, giving him affection, a baby if he wanted it. But he'd finished with the country then and was after a barmaid – Dainty he said her name was and showed round pictures of her, not dainty at all, spreading all over the place.

It's twilight now and Pettie sleeps, and wakes when it is dark. She put the blade back in the razor, not caring if they returned, if they walked into the bathroom while she was at it. She'd get sent to a Borstal, Marji Laye and Sylvie said when she phoned up the woman, but she didn't care about that either. You reach out for a ballpoint, you slip away a counter trinket, or panties or a vest. No one calls out, no one bars your way. She could have said to the old woman that the worms are in the body now; she could have said that all the flowers in the world won't keep the worms out of a body, but no good would come of that.

He wanted to agree about a grandmother being beyond it. Everything they both felt was in his expression and in his eyes. But the old woman has come and what is meant cannot happen until her greed for a baby is taken from the house she has invaded, until her venom ceases, until she isn't there.

★

Sometimes the words Albert removes are scrawled in mammoth letters on the tiled surfaces, sometimes they are cramped, pushed into one another, as if recording a private utterance. Often such attempts at communication are in a language unknown to him, a pattern of strokes and marks that seems like decoration. Strictly speaking, only the tiles are Albert's concern in the Underground stations: to remove as best he can all messages, statements, pronouncements, incitements to violence, abuse of the police authorities, expressions of lust. But he also, for his private satisfaction, erases with a rubber anything in pencil on a nearby poster, any crude additions to figures advertising stage shows or films.

He works on the tiles with cloths and brushes, bottles of erasing liquid, a bucket of soap and water. In the eerie quiet of the night it again outrages his orderly nature that he cannot cleanse the posters as he does the tiles, that it is not his remit to do so, that only the pencilled messages can be rubbed away while bolder obscenities must remain.

Tonight there is the further disappointment that he has failed in his visit to the Dowlers. 'I can't go rodding, this hour,' Mr Dowler crossly protested, misunderstanding and continuing to misunderstand. A smell of beer came from him, specks of foam on the moustache that joined up with his sideburns. A woman's voice called down the stairs, inquiring what the problem was, and Mr Dowler didn't answer and Albert explained that it was Pettie he'd come about. 'Pettie was the girl was looking after your kids, Mr Dowler. Only she made a mistake.' Mr Dowler, still confused, shook his head; Mrs Dowler shouted down again, drawing attention to the time. 'Look, what's your problem, son?' Mr Dowler demanded and Albert repeated what he'd said several times already. 'Listen, son,' Mr Dowler said then, 'you ask that little bitch where the wife's shoes is.' Pettie was wanted by the police, he said, and closed the door.

Eyes smile at Albert from the advertisements that, every night, become his world. Mouths simper, limbs are frozen as they gyrate, words ooze their promise. Black on pale yellow, a scrawl records an experience of Ecstasy. A smiling woman is defiled in two places and Albert tears part of the paper away, bundling it under a seat on the platform. *AIDS the Saviour!* is written, and beside it an account of how a woman was humiliated in a car park. Up Wharfdale the needles are thrown down on the street and in the gutters. There's vomit in the doorways; the girls go by, not seeing you. The time the rent boys turned on him, Little Mister joined in because he was afraid not to.

He bombed . . . She couldn't resist him . . . The message is edged with fire, its urgent letters spread across an explosion, the concrete of buildings a dance of destruction, debris arrested in a night sky. No more than a shadow a man was once, five past three in the morning, stayed down to leave a device after they'd locked the gates.

Albert squeezes dirty water out of his cleaning rags and stares morosely at the scum of bubbles in his bucket. The water that came out of the standpipe at the seed nursery was clean enough, rusty at first but then becoming clear. They should never have left that place. They could have found a Primus stove and done their cooking on it. You see things on skips when you go wandering, no reason why there wouldn't be a Primus stove. He could have got in crisps and more Heinz beans and long-lasting milk and Mother's Pride. They could have bought seeds themselves and grown lettuces and carrots in the tumbled-down glasshouse. They could have got blankets thrown out on a skip.

She'll go up Wharfdale now. What else can happen to a girl without a bed to sleep in? It's fourteen months since Bev went missing. It's a week already since Pettie's been about.

Albert empties the water from his bucket on to the track and replaces his rags and brushes, soap and bucket, in a cupboard on Platform 2. His night's work hardly begun, he climbs up a moving staircase that is stationary now. He'll make up the time, he promises the man who's tidying up around the turnstiles at the top.

The thump of music reaches him as he walks away from the Underground entrance, and when he turns a corner there's a disco's flashing neon, a bouncer with cropped head and stubble belligerent in a doorway. A bigger man than Mr Dowler, he cups the remains of a cigarette in the palm of a hand, a dirty blue T-shirt stretched over his beer-sag. Three girls leave the disco as Albert passes, one pausing to ask the bouncer for a light. A decoration glistens in her nostril as she bends her head over the massive, lazily raised hand. 'Ta,' she says, and for a moment Albert wonders if she's Bev, then sees she isn't. He wonders if Bev would remember him, or pretend she doesn't. Up Wharfdale, Ange pretended once.

Voices from the disco follow him, incomprehensible and loud, beating out the music's rhythm. Leeroy heard voices, Bob Iron and the Metalmen, Ivy On Her Own. Famous, Leeroy said, but no one else at the Morning Star was familiar with Bob Iron and the Metalmen or Ivy On Her Own. A woman in the gas queue said if you hear voices they never go away.

There's no one he knows up Wharfdale when he gets there, not Ange nor Bev, nor Pettie. There are new girls he has never seen before, twelve or thirteen years old. The rent boys are in Samuel Street and Left Street. He stays for a while, then begins the journey back to the streets he prefers. She could be anywhere.

He sits for a while on a low wall, leaning against the wire mesh of a fence. A plane passes over but he can't see what it is. A street light illuminates a notice with a jagged lightning sign: interference with the iron container that the fence protects will result in death.

A man goes by, a white dog running in front of him. He doesn't look at Albert but straight ahead, as if he's nervous of catching a stranger's eye. The dog runs on and he calls it, Tippy, Tippy. She broke her glasses at the Morning Star and they said she'd have to manage for a while. But it was only the side bit and he fixed it to be going on with, a matchstick and Sellotape.

'Come on, Tippy,' the man orders when the dog begins to lick Albert's shoes. 'Sorry about that,' the man says, his head turned sideways, as if he is examining something in the distance, and Albert says it doesn't matter.

He goes on, crossing a common, coming out by the dairy yard he knows, where electric floats are being loaded. 'You got your lot, Sean?' a voice calls out, and there's an incomprehensible reply. Two Indians, one with a suitcase, cross the street to ask him where Caspar Road is, and he says the other side of the dairy yard. Cars pass, going faster than they would in the daytime. A quarter to three it is, the figures luminous on his Zenith. 'I work the Underground nights,' he explained when policemen in a car drew up beside him once. He called the policeman who questioned him sir. He always does that, to be on the safe side. He explained that to Pettie in case she was ever questioned herself, but he doesn't know if she listened.

Across the street a grey, gaunt building with wide steps is lit up, its open door revealing uniformed figures in a hallway. Albert pauses, as he often does here: the women of the Salvation Army are congregating for their soup run, a few of their male colleagues standing by in case protection is necessary. The figures move or stand still in conversation, heads bent close, gestures made. They're quiet people, Albert considers, except when a hymn is called for. More than ever, in his defeated mood tonight, he wants to be one of them, to wear their regimental colours, to be told what to do and then to do it.

Another plane goes over, lights flashing on its wing tips.

The woman who was humiliated in the car park comes into his thoughts; he wonders if she lived or died. Joey Ells could have died, Miss Rapp said, even without water in the tank; it stood to reason she'd slip, the steps half gone, the slime. He wonders where Miss Rapp is now. 'Rapp's off,' Joe Minching said the day she packed her bags. Mrs Hoates went pale as putty the time Joey Ells broke her legs, but then she was herself again. Bev's probably dead.

It wouldn't surprise him if Miss Rapp has joined the Army, if at this very minute she's going out on a soup run. Albert nods to himself and sees Miss Rapp, gangling and scrawny, her hair untidy, in the woman's version of the red and blue uniform he covets. He'd like it, being able to talk to Miss Rapp again, to tell her how it wasn't all that nice when people laughed at the big man on the streets, and that Mrs Biddle is afraid to open her door to callers in case the social services attempt to counsel her, that Pettie's in a plight. He hears the music and the tramp of feet and sees himself walking beside Miss Rapp, both of them in the red and blue. In the end they talk only about Pettie, sharing the worry.

★

She fears the dog may roam at night, but there is only silence when she listens. The air is colder than it was. The stillness is different from the stillness of the lanes and fields.

Cautiously she pushes open the door in the wall. If the dog comes she'll call its name and pat its head, the same's she's done a dozen times. But only a black cat darts from her path.

A fading moonlight casts grey shadows in the greyness before dawn begins its mellowing of the house's bulk.

Windows gleam then, curtains showing in some. Contours sharpen, trees and shrubs reclaim their colours. Lawns do not come green, but an insipid yellow. Borders and heather slopes lighten. Rooks scavenge for leather-jackets.

In the summer-house there are deckchairs against a wall, croquet mallets and croquet balls, a slatted table folded with the chairs, sun-glasses on a windowsill, a tray with Gordon's gin and other bottles on it, a coloured umbrella in a corner. Outside, on a white iron table, its round surface an openwork pattern of flattened roses, two empty glasses have each attracted a wasp, motionless now. Near the brick-sided cold-frames, potatoes have been dug, their haulm withered on the dry earth.

She pokes about the cobbled yard. There is the car she has seen the couple in; *Subaru* it says on it, *Justy.* The other car is his – the one that in a dream he drew up beside her, near the graveyard. There's nothing of the old woman's anywhere, neither a car nor anything else.

At half past six the post van comes. She leaves the garden then, to watch from the doorway in the wall, and sees the first curtains pulled back. At twenty past seven a newspaper is pushed through the front-door letterbox, another brought round to the back. At five past eight a milk float comes; voices speak in the yard. The dog lollops up to her to sniff damply at her legs, then pads off to the ragged grass beneath the trees.

Hungry now, Pettie remains. The woman in black clothes crosses the yard. The hall door opens and is left like that.

Anyone could slip into the house. Anyone could pass through the hall, could take possession of the silver fowls on the dining-room table and then skulk away. It is typical of him that he doesn't think of that, typical of the person he is.

When he appears she wants to go to him, to say she knows he has guessed there wasn't ever a ring, to tell him all the truth. But no good would come of that, and instead she watches while he carries a deckchair from the summer-house. The old woman spreads her familiar, differently coloured rug on the grass and moves the chair he has erected for her. He goes to the house and returns with his baby.

While miles away, all morning, a chain-saw whines, Pettie watches the woman she has come to hate. She watches her turning the pages of her book, standing up to attend to some need of the baby's, then settling herself in her chair again. She has a white hat on, wide-brimmed, to protect her from the sun, and dark glasses to protect her eyes. Her head droops once or twice, but then she is alert again.

Calm now and yet excited, unaffected by her hunger, Pettie waits, but all that day the moment does not come.

9

Four days go by, during which Maidment is unaware that his eavesdropper's role is shared. Nor does Zenobia know that she is regularly observed lingering in the sunshine after gathering herbs. Thaddeus is ignorant of a passion that will not be stilled. Mrs Iveson knows nothing of her detestation. Her death in midday sunshine, her death in the dark of night, coming to her in sleep, her death most suddenly in the hall, on the landing, on the stairs, catching her naked in her bath, touching a half-spoken word, arresting the movement of an arm: she does not know this has been real, before it shrivelled away to nothing. She does not know a greater reality remains, a single chance that gathers strength with time.

Over lunch on the fifth of the days that pass – consommé, oatcakes, cheese, coffee – the conversation in the dining-room, usually conducted along similar meal-time lines, includes a variation.

'I'm glad I came,' Mrs Iveson confesses, seeking to convey more than the words imply, yet not too much.

'And I am that you did.'

'Are you, Thaddeus?'

He smiles and reassures her. Listening, she wonders if her daughter knew him better than she does now. Or was there always, for Letitia too, a reticence that is the shell of his protection? Mystery in a person is attractive: more often than not it is its presence that inspires the helpless, tumbling descent into love. When Thaddeus was a stranger to her, as he was before this summer, it was always incomprehensible that Letitia appeared to sense something of the mysterious in him: it is less so now. Mrs Iveson cannot tell her son-in-law that she likes him better, although he knows, of course, that once she did not like him at all. To say what she has said already is as far as she can go today, and probably ever.

'We haven't quarrelled.' Thaddeus smiles away the word that doesn't belong, for it is ludicrous that they should quarrel, neither by nature being the kind to. He wonders if she knows that, for his part, he nurtures no animosity towards her and never has, although aware of her misgivings as regards himself. 'I doubt we ever shall,' he adds, preferring to say that than to touch upon his feelings.

'When I first suggested a nanny for Georgina, and later when I suggested our present arrangement, I felt you could not at all have managed. Perhaps, though, you could have.'

'It's better for Georgina to have someone as a mother.'

'If it's a strain, you must say.'

'And of course so must you.'

'All this is much more than something for me to do. It is everything, but that should not come into it.'

'It does come into it, because you are who you are, because Georgina is your child too.'

They hover, like uncertain birds. They skirt emotion, steer clear of words that might drag it out of hiding. Thaddeus's hands are occupied, slicing cheese, his concentration guiding the slow movement of the knife. Her eyes unwavering, fixed now on the sliver cut from the Etorki, Mrs Iveson does not speak. Then, suddenly, she says:

'You made Letitia happy.'

'Don't people in marriages try for that?'

'People in marriages are often wretched.'

Cautious again, they do not say more. On the table in the hall the telephone rings and Maidment, passing with the coffee, settles the tray on the table's edge, one hand still holding it. As he lifts the receiver he wonders if – as several times recently and still a puzzle – there will be no response when he speaks. But a woman's voice says at once:

'Mr Davenant?'

When Thaddeus comes the same voice tells him that Mrs Dorothy Ferry has asked if he might be contacted and informed of her admission.

'Admission?'

The name of a hospital is given. 'Mrs Ferry's comfortable, Mr Davenant, but there is cause for some concern. I rang at once.'

'That was very good of you. Thank you.'

'I'll give you our address, sir.'

'Yes. Please do.'

He listens and is told, informed that in the circumstances he may come at any time. Directions are given, should he care to do so. 'This afternoon would not be inconvenient for us, Mr Davenant.'

'There is some urgency?'

'We would not advise delay, sir.'

In the dining-room, when the conversation as it was is not resumed, Thaddeus says he'll be out for a bit, explaining that someone has been taken into hospital, not giving details.

'I'm sorry.'

'Yes, so am I.' And he wonders as he speaks if once

he would have so promptly agreed to make this journey. Reflecting further, he knows he would not; and knows that making it now is another response to the influence of death and the sentiment it trails.

Twenty minutes later, hanging clothes on the line in the yard, Zenobia sees the blue Saab backed out of the garage. Through glass and vine leaves, drawing on his after-lunch cigarette behind the conservatory, Maidment observes it halt for a moment on the tarmac sweep, the passenger door pushed open. On her way from the dining-room, Mrs Iveson hears Rosie called.

The hum of the engine fades and then can not be heard. Pettie listens for the sound of the car returning – something forgotten or some sudden change of plan. But nothing disturbs this dead time of the afternoon.

★

'My dear!' Mrs Ferry greets her visitor from bright white pillows, her effort at jauntiness collapsing before it has a chance. 'My dear, I didn't think you'd come.'

Her voice is weak, a croak that is a whisper also. She tries to smile. She pushes out a hand.

'It's homey here,' she says. 'A little place is.'

'Yes, I noticed.'

'Can't stand the big ones.'

'I'm sorry you're not well, Dot.'

'Dear, I haven't been, you know.'

'You said.'

'You didn't go along with it.'

'Of course I did.'

'I couldn't blame you, dear.'

Again there is the effort at a smile, but something collapses

136

in Mrs Ferry's face and from beneath closed eyelids tears run on cheeks that are innocent of make-up, the first time Thaddeus has ever seen them so.

'You rest now, Dot. Don't try to talk.'

'A pity we didn't tie our loose ends together. A pity we didn't get round to it.'

Her voice fades, is hardly audible when it returns, solitary words rising out of a jumble to hang there meaninglessly, the names of men, items on the menu at the Beech Trees, childhood words. In the small hospital they have given her a room to herself, to which a nurse now brings two cups of tea. She takes one away, realizing at once that her patient cannot manage it. When Thaddeus has drunk some of his he says:

'I think you'd like to have a sleep.'

'You pour us a drink, dear? He has to see the tax man. He won't be back.'

Children are playing somewhere, a distant sound, muffled by double-glazing.

'Come back to bed, Thad.'

A sister bustles in, brisk and jolly, her manner filling the little room. She takes Mrs Ferry's pulse. 'Lovely,' she says, then motions Thaddeus to the door. 'Your mother's quite poorly,' she says more quietly.

'Actually she's not my mother.'

'Oh, I thought they said – a friend, are you?'

'Yes.'

'She's not too bright. There's been sedation, of course.'

'I understand.'

'She'll know more about herself when she's had a sleep. She lives on her own, we're to understand?'

'Yes, she's on her own.'

'You can always tell. I'm sorry about that little error.'

'I'll go in a moment.'

The sister nods and goes herself. Mrs Ferry's murmuring continues when Thaddeus returns to her bedside. It ceases when she opens her eyes. Slowly a smile begins, then wearily languishes.

'Your wife,' she says. 'I often think about that kindness.'

'I'm a widower, Dot. I wanted to tell you that.'

'A what?'

'A widower.'

'Never, dear. He married a Lytham lady. Still clonking along, the pair of them.'

'No, Dot, it's –'

'June eighty-eight, the registry in Lytham. Funny, how some people make a go of it.'

She closes her eyes, then with an effort opens them again.

'The pancreas. They say – it's not so good.'

'It'll be all right, Dot.'

'You'll take me to your lovely home, will you? Will you, Thad? I always wanted that.'

'Of course.'

'Butter side up, Thad. I always knew you'd settle butter side up. I used to say to Oscar, I said to Chef. "Good-looking boy," Chef said. Well, you know what Chef got up to.'

Thaddeus doesn't, but nods all the same.

'It's final, you know,' Mrs Ferry murmurs. 'You know that, Thad? This lovely summer and it's final.'

'Of course it isn't.'

'I liked it best at Blackpool. I never thought I'd like a

place like Blackpool, but I did. Time we were naughties there, you and I.'

He does not deny the claim, only wondering if for the moment he is someone else for her, or if the confusion's in her memory.

'I wanted you, Thad. Oh, my dear, I wanted you so.'

'You had me.'

'Not ever. A boy you were. To this day, Thad. Pour us a drink, dear.'

'In a moment. Just rest a while.'

'You think he knows? You think they told him? The day he married me he said he was the luckiest man on earth and all I did was lead him a dance. You tell him that from me? You tell him I'm sorry, Thad?'

'Of course.'

'Like yesterday, Blackpool seems. But then again it isn't, is it?'

'Not quite.'

'Well, there you go, as they say.'

'You rest now, Dot.'

'Your lovely house, your lovely wife. I'm happy for you, Thad.'

Her head drops back, a dribble runs from one corner of her mouth. Alarmed, Thaddeus presses the bell that hangs near the pillow.

'She's sleeping now,' the nurse who comes says.

★

Rosie noses about the hospital car park. Leaning against the side of the car, he lets her for a while. Butter side up, and of course that's true. Why could he never have been less elusive, less private with a woman who so longed for him to be forthcoming? As she lay there now he could not even say that his garden is suffering from the drought, nor that his mother-in-law has come to his house, that he and she – old enemies – are determined to create a family of a kind and that, for both of them, there is the beginning of recovery after the shock of death. He is ashamed he could confess today to being a widower when he could not before.

The guilt that shadows a relationship accompanies him on the drive home, still hanging about his thoughts when he leaves the traffic behind. Not far from Quincunx a rabbit scuttles from one thorn hedge to the other and he slows down to avoid it, even though rabbits are a nuisance in the garden.

10

'No, that's Mr Davenant I'd think,' Maidment says in the drawing-room.

He speaks soothingly, standing over her, looking down at her. She is huddled on the sofa, one hand grasping the other in an effort to prevent their shaking. Rosie is in the garden again, having given her single, staccato bark. A door closes, and there are Thaddeus's footsteps in the hall and then he's in the room.

'The child's been taken, sir,' she hears Maidment saying, and Thaddeus saying Zenobia has told him already. Thaddeus asks what happened exactly and she says it was her fault. While she's speaking there is the sound of another car.

'When I woke up Georgina wasn't there,' she says.

Maidment goes before the doorbell summons him. The hall door opens and there are voices. Thaddeus's tone is expressionless when he asks again what happened.

'I fell asleep,' she says.

The police officers are two men and a woman. Unable to prevent herself, she wonders if they're the ones who came before, their presence now connecting the two events. The two events belong together, an insistence hammers in her brain: if Letitia had not died this would not be happening now. That makes no sense, yet already has gathered a rationality of its own.

'Mr Davenant?' one of the officers greets Thaddeus. He

is a bulky, dishevelled man, not in uniform, the frayed part of his tie half hidden in its knot. The tie is red and green, held in place with a tiepin. There's a trace of cigarette ash on the brown of his jacket.

'Yes,' Thaddeus says.

She looks up to nod when Thaddeus says who she is. She says again it was her fault.

'No one's fault, ma'am, something like this.' The policeman shakes his head, his tone tiredly sympathetic. She can feel him wanting to sigh; she knows he blames her. Old, he's thinking, trying not to let it show. 'Let's just sort out the facts,' he says.

None of the three sits down, although Thaddeus has indicated that they should. The uniformed man is short-haired, in early middle age, a finger missing from his left hand. The woman is much younger, and smarter in appearance, her blue uniform freshly pressed. A poor skin well disguised, Maidment observed when he opened the hall door, but Mrs Iveson doesn't notice that.

'Is there anyone you can think of?' The man who is not in uniform continues to be in charge, the short-haired one fiddling with some kind of recording gadget or bleeper, she can't tell which.

Thaddeus shakes his head. He says he has only minutes ago returned to the house. Then he turns to her.

'Please tell us.' He looks down at her, his voice calm, as if he wishes to be soothing, as Maidment was a moment ago. She thought it was a dream when she awoke and saw the rug empty but for the toys and the carry-cot on it. She stood up and looked around her. She stared at the rug and the toys and the carry-cot, feeling she was still in a dream.

'I ran about the garden like a mad creature, calling Georgina's name over and over again. I went on calling out, thinking she had crawled away. But of course that was ridiculous.'

'And there is no one either of you can think of?' Patiently the question is posed again. And then: 'The child's mother is not here, sir?'

Mrs Iveson closes her eyes; again there is the feeling that she is in a dream. Thaddeus says he is widowed.

'I see, sir.'

Relentlessly, or so it seems to Mrs Iveson, the man goes on. His colleagues are not wearing jackets, but he has made no concession to the heat of the afternoon. His untidy brown suit is heavy and wintry-looking.

'There's no one who could have an interest in the child, sir?'

'No.'

For a moment, when the Maidments brought her into the house, she found it hard to speak. Maidment suggested brandy but she didn't want it. When he was on the telephone she asked Zenobia what time it was.

'And you can think of no one, madam?'

'No.'

The young policewoman silently condoles, her gaze lowered to her plain black shoes, then moving over the polished boards of the floor, then raised again. She cannot offer pity in a smile; it would not do to smile. WPC Denise Flynn she was introduced as.

'When you dozed, madam –'

'I slept for longer than I thought. When I woke up I thought maybe a minute or two. But it was half an hour, perhaps three-quarters even. I didn't know that until Zenobia brought me in from the garden, until I asked what time it was.'

'And there was nothing unusual when you looked about the garden, madam? Nothing that struck you?'

'Only that Georgina wasn't there any more.'

'Is it a regular thing for you to sit out in that particular place in the afternoon? With the baby?'

'Yes, it has been.'

'Every day?'

'Yes.'

'You show me, madam? If you would.'

They stand at the french windows. She points at the deckchair and the rug beneath the catalpa tree. WPC Denise Flynn steps out on to the paving outside, then hurries on the upper lawn. Bounding about around her, Rosie drops her ball, then picks it up and drops it again.

'That dog all right, sir?' the man in uniform asks sharply, the first time he has spoken, and Thaddeus says Rosie's all right.

'He wasn't here, did you say, sir?' the other man inquires. 'The dog was out with you?'

'Yes, she was.'

'And you were gone, how long, sir?'

'A couple of hours.'

'Out for a walk, sir?'

'No. We were in the car.'

Something stirs in Mrs Iveson's consciousness, a sense of experiencing, not long ago, questioning like this. Having pointed at the deckchair in which she fell asleep, she hasn't sat down again. She stands between the two french windows, the fingertips of her left hand lightly touching the surface of the table with Letitia's photograph on it. She doesn't feel groggy any more, but that support is there if she needs it. Inspector Ogle, it suddenly comes to her: Inspector Henry Ogle asked questions like the ones the present man is asking, and there was something he wasn't satisfied about with Miss Amble's replies. That was happening when she dropped off.

'The gentleman who let us in, sir. Is he – he would look after things here, sir?'

'Maidment and his wife are employed in the house.'

'And did the Maidments look for the child, madam, when they heard your distress?'

'Maidment did. I told him to. We knew then Georgina couldn't possibly have crawled away, but he looked all the same. He even went down the drive.'

'And before that you were aware, Mrs Iveson, of no vehicle drawing away from the drive? Nothing like that?'

'No.'

The policewoman returns. She doesn't shake her head, or comment. The man who isn't asking the questions glances at her but there is no exchange, not even of a look.

'I came here,' Mrs Iveson says, 'to look after Georgina. We were going to have a nanny, but we changed our minds.'

It isn't relevant. She doesn't know why she volunteered information not prompted by a question. She sees herself for a moment, dropping off in her deckchair, old and stupid, not up to a simple task. No matter what their shortcomings, the girls they interviewed would not have fallen asleep.

'We have an alert out, of course,' the man says. 'That was

145

relayed at once. May I ask, sir, if it is a usual practice for you to take the dog with you in the car at that time of day? Are you normally away, sir, of an afternoon?'

'I'm almost always here.'

The man nods, with what seems like satisfaction. By the look of things, he concludes aloud, today was chosen specially.

'Notice anyone about the place, sir? Hanging about, even a while back, madam?'

They both say no, are asked to think for a moment, and then say no again.

'My wife was well off,' Thaddeus adds.

'And that is generally known, sir? Locally?'

'I think it probably is.'

'If we might question your couple now, sir?'

The room goes silent when Thaddeus leads them from it. She gazes across mallows and garish cosmos at the empty deckchair, her book on the grass beside it. Her reading glasses are there too, although she cannot see them.

'A telephone call may come,' Thaddeus says, returning. 'We are not to answer it until there's been time for one of them to get to an extension.'

'They think Georgina's been kidnapped?' The word, so often encountered in the novels she reads, so often heard on the radio and the television, and come across in newspapers, feels alien on her lips. 'A ransom demand?' she says, and it sounds absurd.

'Yes, that's what they mean.'

'We must pay, Thaddeus.'

'They say we mustn't.'

She moves across the room, to sit again on the sofa.

'We have the money. What does it matter, parting with it?'

'More likely, they say, tomorrow's post will bring a note. More likely than a phone call. But they say you never know.'

Did the two who were so silent in the drawing-room contribute something to the conversation on the way to the kitchen, or is this just Thaddeus's way of putting it? She wonders, caught up with an unimportant detail, unable for a moment to shake it off, and then it goes.

'I should at least have heard a car.'

'I doubt it would have driven up. The Maidments heard nothing either.'

'Negligent is what they'll say.'

'No, I don't think so.'

He says something else, she does not listen.

'My God, how could I have?' she whispers, and there is silence in the room again.

★

'From a window,' Maidment says. 'I happened to be passing. I happened to look out.'

'And when was this, sir?'

'The day the knives came back.' Maidment turns to his wife. 'Thursday week, was it?'

'It was Thursday week the knives came back.' And Zenobia adds for the policeman's benefit: 'The kitchen knives resharpened.'

'And what exactly did you see, sir?'

'Nothing, to tell the truth. It was the dog drew my attention.'

'And why was that, Mr Maidment?'

'The dog was interested, but I couldn't ascertain why. Her tail was going.'

'Your view was obscured, sir?'

'It's a long way off. You have to see through trees.'

'And we're to presume Mr Davenant himself was elsewhere at the time? And the lady also?'

'They were in the house.'

'But although you didn't actually see anyone you formed the impression that there was someone there because the dog was wagging her tail?'

'He thought he noticed a movement,' Zenobia answers for her husband. 'He said it later. No more than some disturbance, he said.'

'And this is where in the garden?'

'There's a door in the wall. An archway with wistaria, beyond the plum trees.'

Hearing this, the two uniformed officers leave the kitchen. 'Nothing like that today?' their superior pursues his questioning when they have gone. 'Nothing out of the way?'

'Nothing.'

Maidment responds at once, Zenobia after a moment's thought. 'Nothing,' she says too.

'Did you report the Thursday sighting in the garden, sir?'

'How d'you mean, report?'

'Did you mention it to Mr Davenant?'

'There wasn't much to report. In a manner of speaking.'

'He said he would mention it,' Zenobia intervenes, 'if he had a suspicion that anyone came in by that door another time.'

'It's unusual, is it, for people to come into the garden this way?'

Unusual for an outsider, Zenobia agrees, and Maidment adds:

'Mr Davenant slips in and out on the odd occasion, and Mrs Davenant did in her time. Taking the dog down to the stream.'

'This door leads to the stream?'

'There's a path by the edge of the fields, going by the spinney to the lane. Or you can go on straight down to the stream.'

'And people use this path?'

'Not much.'

It was a short-cut from the house in days gone by, Zenobia says. 'It seems they went to church that way if they wanted to walk in summer.'

'So it's not your experience, sir, that a passer-by might open that door and come into the garden, maybe making a mistake?'

'Never.'

Zenobia points out that a passer-by would have no right. Sometimes a cat comes into the garden. Or a dog, not on a leash, is called back from the drive. Now and again a car comes up the drive, and goes away when it is realized that this is the wrong house. That's not often, probably less than once a year.

'Mr Davenant's a widower, I understand?'

Surprised, Zenobia wonders why this is mentioned. The way he puts it, the man knows already. Everything like that would have been established in the drawing-room. Maidment says:

'There was a road accident. Not long ago.'

The policeman nods. A flicker of interest passes through his expression, a frown gathers and then is gone. The news was broken by the police, Maidment says. The news about that accident.

Listening to her husband giving the details, Zenobia is aware of the same sense of connection that Mrs Iveson has experienced in the drawing-room, and it feels like mockery to her that there should be this second cruelty, drifting out of the summer blue, as the first did. Maidment's thoughts are similar, then are invaded by a famous episode in the past – the taking of the Lindbergh baby. It was before his time; what he recalls is hearsay, supplied to him by an elderly butler of the old school who enjoyed such titbits. If that's what this is there'll be a message in the morning, the words cut out of a newspaper and pasted up: used banknotes to be secreted in a rubbish bin or a telephone-box or the cistern of a public lavatory, a specified place, a specified time.

'If contact is made after we're gone,' the policeman says, 'I've told Mr Davenant and the lady we'll need to know at once. While we're still here don't answer the phone until we're in a position to monitor the call.'

'You think they're after money?' Zenobia inquires, and hears that at this stage it's important to keep an open mind.

'It's equally possible we could be looking for a local woman. Is there anyone at all you can think of, a woman who got to know the routine of the house through observation? A frustrated would-be mother, an older woman it often is, though by no means always. Someone who saw the opportunity and took her chance?'

There's no one they can think of, but for Zenobia the

thought of a woman taking her chance is preferable to brutish men. Years ago at Oakham Manor a gang got in. They silenced the alarm and poked a kitchen grab through a fanlight, drawing back the bolts with it, even lifting the key from the lock. Every scrap of silver gone, and never established how it was they knew where to look for it. Zenobia still shivers with apprehension at the thought of men with shaved heads roaming about a house at night. It was she who found the back door swinging the next morning, she confides to the bulky policeman, and had to break the news on the telephone to the Hadleighs, in Austria at the time.

'Yes, it's unpleasant, Mrs Maidment. But I'm afraid what we have here is more unpleasant still, no matter who's responsible. So no local person comes to mind?'

'No one at all.'

'I'd hardly say it was local,' Maidment contributes. 'I'd lay my bones down there's money in this somewhere.'

Zenobia notices a moment of surprise in the policeman's features, occasioned by the expression used, but when he speaks he is impassive again.

'As I say, sir, we have to keep an open mind. But of recent times it's been women who've been helping themselves to babies.' A while back, they may remember, a baby born only a few hours was taken from a hospital ward. Another time, a baby-minder who ran off in Camden came to light in County Limerick. In this day and age, if a woman has a fancy for a baby she takes what's going.

'Even so,' Maidment persists, 'I'd say we're talking ransom money.'

'That's not discounted, sir.'

'We had those phone calls,' Zenobia says, suddenly remembering.

'And what were they, Mrs Maidment?'

'Someone ringing up and not saying anything.'

'When was this?'

'They began a couple of weeks back. You'd answer and the receiver'd be put down.'

'I see.'

WPC Denise Flynn and her colleague return. The door in the wall was open, Denise Flynn reports, not wide, but a little. The ground's too hard to carry footprints, her colleague says.

'Usually open, that door, Mr Maidment?'

'Never.'

'Most likely that's the way they came and went. A couple it could be.'

★

The rooks swirl above the oaks and the house. Climbing or diving, they caw and screech, observed by two silent buzzards, motionless in the air. Below them, another police car arrives.

The garden is searched for a sign left behind by an intruder or intruders, but there is nothing. Local houses are visited. Increasingly favoured is the theory that a motherless baby has become the prey of a woman with an obsession about her own maternal needs. In low voices the likelihood is repeated in the police cars as evening settles over lanes and fields, and the inmates of farmhouses and cottages are disturbed.

'Yes, it may be that,' Thaddeus agrees when the notion about a woman of the neighbourhood is put to him. There is nothing he can add. He has known the women of the neighbourhood all his life. Some he has known as children, seen them becoming girls, those same girls marrying and having children of their own. When asked about the peculiar or the unusual among them, he mentions Mrs Parch, who claims to possess the power of healing, who has been making a profit from the exercise of her skill for sixty years. Visitors still come to her cottage to receive the benefit of her gifted hands and to hear her daughter, Hilda, read a report in a local paper when the phenomenon was contemporaneously recorded. Hilda herself has chalked up a success or two with herbal remedies: a decoction of grasses and the juice extracted from comfrey for gastric ailments and arthritic joints. But neither Mrs Parch nor her daughter interests WPC Denise Flynn, who has been assigned the task of gathering information about the women of the locality.

'There's Abbie Mates,' Thaddeus remembers also. A younger woman, a fortune-teller at summer fêtes, reader of the Tarot cards. And there's Melanie, who lives alone by an old railway crossing and regularly bears the children of a man who visits her. But they, too, fail to arouse the policewoman's suspicions.

Further questioning reveals that among the house's usual visitors two charity women came recently for Letitia's clothes, and Jehovah's Witnesses have been, and a girl to search for a ring she dropped. Hoping to get rid of a load of tar, a man called in, offering to resurface the drive at a bargain price. Burly, black-haired, a stutter coming on when his sales pitch became excited: every detail remembered is of interest and is recorded. 'They showed you literature and that?' WPC Denise Flynn prompts. 'The Witnesses?' And bleakly Thaddeus nods.

The white police cars go eventually, with fresh instructions left about a possible telephone communication. 'Someone knew,' Zenobia concludes in the kitchen. 'Someone knew we have an afternoon rest ourselves, and saw the car drive off.' She blames herself, as Mrs Iveson does, but Maidment is dismissive of any misdemeanour on his wife's part or on his. Half an hour only they lie down for, he reminds Zenobia, and in the half-hour today he didn't close an eyelid. The newspaper dropped to the floor, he grants her that, but he did not sleep. Anything untoward he would have heard.

It is dark in the bathroom that once was Mr and Mrs
Hoates's. The window is boarded; outside it is almost night.
She has fed Georgina Belle and Georgina Belle is now
asleep. It is quiet except, somewhere and occasionally, there
is a scrabbling of mice.

Pettie herself will not sleep tonight, although she is tired
and feels she wouldn't mind a whole week of sleeping, just
lying there. It wasn't like the taking of the ballpoint, the
stool pulled out for the man to stand on, the reaching
down of the chocolate box. It wasn't like the taking of
the make-up tubes the time she almost dropped one, or
the little black clocks, or taking the scarf with the horses'
heads on it, or the earrings and the brooch a week ago.
Excitement made her shiver when she crossed the grass and
could be seen from the windows, when she lifted Georgina
Belle and the woman didn't move, when Georgina Belle
didn't wake up either. And when she hurried on the way
through the fields, and by the houses and there was still no
one about, her breath was heavy with relief. But then
the children were there, playing some kind of game on the
towpath, and when she tried to put the dummy in it was
too late.

She wonders what's happening now in the house where
she has so longed to be with him. No way he won't be
remembering what she said about a grandmother, no way

he won't be regretting he didn't listen at the time. All that is perfectly as she planned, and taking things into her possession has always been what she can do, what she is good at and still was today, her skill, as the man she sells stuff to says. If the children hadn't stopped and stared when their noise woke up Georgina Belle she'd have gone by and they wouldn't have known. Never before were there children playing on the towpath.

She should have taken her glasses off, she should have kept her head turned away. She should have put the dummy in before ever there was a need for it. The children would be asked. No way they wouldn't say they heard a whimpering.

In the car park where the towpath came out she walked by the phone-box from which she'd planned to dial 999, every syllable of what she had to say practised and perfect: a woman acting underhand with a baby, a grey-haired, thin-faced woman with a lazy eye, who put the baby by the basins in the car-park toilets, who hurried off when she realized she was followed by someone who'd been suspicious. 'I come back to look for my finger-ring in the lane. I was by the pillars either side of the drive and saw her. I followed her because it was a baby she was trying to hide. I knew it was Georgina Belle.' But the children would say there never was a woman with a lazy eye.

In the dark Pettie tries to repair the reality she is left with. She could go out now and phone him up, not bothering with 999 because it's too late for that. She could ask to speak to him if someone else answered, and then explain – how she ran away in a panic from the car park when she saw the woman still hanging about. 'All I thought to do was take

Georgina Belle to a place of safety, Mr Davenant.' She could trust to luck that they wouldn't bother with the children, now that they knew.

Pettie goes over that. 'What I thought was she'll snatch her from me when I'm getting her back to your house, sir. Like on the towpath or in the fields.' She hears his sigh of relief, and her own voice saying it was only lucky she came out that afternoon to look for her finger-ring where she hadn't looked properly before.

But the children heard the whimpering and already they'll have said. Squatting on the dirty floorboards of the bathroom, again she tries to find a way, but again knows that from the moment the children stopped to stare there never was one.

She lights a match and then a cigarette. 'Wife and kiddies,' Joe Minching said; and the rictus began in the fisherman's face; and they said she was to blame when Eric wasn't in Ikon Floor Coverings any more, they said she should be taken in. In the brief illumination, pipes hang from the walls where bath and wash-basin have been crudely disconnected before being taken away. A mirror has been shattered, its fragments in a corner. All the whimpering in the world, all the crying and screaming won't attract attention here, as now and again it did at the Dowlers' and the Fennertys'.

When the cigarette is finished Pettie lights another and then another, the flare of the match each time flickering on the sleeping face of the baby she has taken. While the last match is still alight she gently places the dummy – once Darren Fennerty's – between the slightly open lips. In the dark she makes a butterfly and places it where it will be something for Georgina Belle to look at later, when light comes through the cracks between the window boards.

Then Pettie goes, closing the bathroom door behind her.

In the dining-room the dinner table has been laid, but no food is eaten. Much later, in the drawing-room, not huddled now but straight-backed in an armchair, Mrs Iveson can hardly see her son-in-law when he comes in because she has not turned on the lights. She watched him in the garden before darkness fell – among the birch trees and the plum trees, by the summer-house, pacing slowly around the lawns, stooping now and again to pull a weed out from a flower-bed. He says nothing when he comes in, and she wonders at first if he knows she's there. Rosie is with him and settles down, pressed against her legs.

'I'm sorry, Thaddeus.'

He stands still in the gloom. She senses the shaking of his head, but does not see it. Time seems not to be passing, even though the evening has darkened so, even though the clock in the hall has chimed the hours and half-hours.

'I'm sorry.'

He still says nothing. In the hall the telephone rings and he goes to answer it. 'Yes,' she hears him say. 'Yes.' He listens and then says thank you, listens again and says good-night. She can tell it isn't what it might have been.

'Of course it wasn't your fault,' he says, returning. 'Of course not.'

He doesn't stay, and a few minutes later she hears his car drive away and wonders what he hopes for. 'We've called her Georgina,' Letitia told her father in St Bee's, and then repeated that, twice or three times. But it never impinged. The last time they visited St Bee's a shaft of sunlight kept catching the blue stripes of the tie that was always so very tidily knotted. Sharp as a card, the tip of a handkerchief protruded from the outside breast pocket and she thought of a figure in a shop window. How fortunate, she tells herself, he is tonight.

*

Thaddeus struggles against thought while flat suburbs spread about him. Ribbons of development are broken, then begin again; dormitory settlements give way to mouldering ware-houses, waterworks stretch for half a mile. Bombsites have not been built on, used-car lots are fenced with high wire mesh. Streets are straight and short, Victorian brick.

A woman with a baby hurries on none of them, no abandoned bundle fills a darkened corner. 'She asked that you be informed,' the voice of the hospital sister interrupted his silent plea that the telephone call would bring some other news. 'A merciful release, we can only say.' And he thought yes, a merciful release, and hardly knew.

Again, as best he can, he veils the images that have recently brought him solace but are painful now: Georgina just born, Letitia's smiling tiredness, his own hands reaching out; Georgina when he saw her last, sleeping in her nursery after lunch. Ahead of him, lit up and open, a public house is called the Old Edward, and for a moment he is tempted to enter it, to talk to its landlord or some woman across a grimy bar, to be someone else and have someone else's thoughts. For an hour or so yet he could drink and in the end be drunk and know oblivion.

'We'll go, Tadzio': his mother saying that comes back, as if from her limbo she seeks in this cruel time to make amends, to rescue from it the child she never knew a man, nor ever knew at all. Through Metz and Kaiserslautern and Berlin, her long white finger first traced their journey to the country he had invented from her scraps: ships and sails on a frozen sea, her remembered street lamps of brightly decorated metal, coal dug out with a spade. *Eva Paczkowska* she showed him, handwritten on a certificate he could not understand, and in a photograph she pointed at the house where she'd been born. At a café table she had looked up and for the first time saw his father, his fur hat on a table by a coffee percolator, his hands held back from the red-hot metal of a stove. 'Tadzio, you were born that day.' Born because of the love that began in the fug of a coffee house, because his father had come to her cold, dark country to sell soap.

'Look, Tadzio!' But it was still his father, not he, she pointed for – at St Hyacinthus' Church, at all the sights of Lazienki. 'Palaces! Palaces!' his father had exclaimed. 'How many more, for heaven's sake!' The Blue, the Primate's, the Archbishop's, the Pac, the Raczyński, the Krasiński, the Palace upon the Water. '*Kanapka*,' an old sandwich-seller offered, opening a sandwich to display its contents, which years ago she had done for his father too. There was the restaurant where his father first ate *naleśniki*, the florid waiter no more than sixteen then. 'Oh, what happiness it was!' And strangers in Eva Paczkowska's city listened to the story of the Englishman who once came to Poland, who gave a Polish girl, in return for Poland's gift to him, a quiet English house, cherry trees at each corner of a garden.

Thaddeus passes the Old Edward by. He tries to hear his mother saying a tailor sat cross-legged in that window, to hear her telling him that *jajko* is egg and *kawa* coffee, making him repeat *Górale mieszkają w górach*. But the distraction does not hold. Still warm, the air is drily odorous, a smell of old dust and buildings. Litter has gathered in the gutters and neglected doorways. Street lights are dim, as if the neighbourhood deserves no better.

He has not come to this nowhere place with hope, but only to escape all that his house is now. Tonight it's inconsequential that his beautiful mother used up her love in comforting an invalid of misfortune and of war. Or that his father sighed and only wished to be alone with her, his body shivering in a bout of pain.

Divers will go down. They'll go down to the murk, to old prams and supermarket trolleys, wheels of bicycles, parts of cars, the rotting shells of boats. In their ugly wet-suits they'll search the slime, fish streaking about them, dead flotsam disturbed. They'll root among the weeds and clumps of rust. They'll lay out rags of clothing on the riverbank and gaze at them, and nod.

Thaddeus calculates: his child has lived for a hundred and eighty-eight days.

★

A ladder was placed beneath the nursery window; in a matter of minutes the baby was gone. When he heard, Al Capone offered a reward, knowing how he'd feel himself, he said. Twenty-five thousand dollars Lindbergh earned for flying the Atlantic, common knowledge at the time.

'I would ask you not to,' Zenobia requests. 'It doesn't help.'

A riposte comes swiftly to her husband's lips but is not issued. An hour ago, when he walked to the end of the drive, he saw the lights of two police cars parked a few yards away and there was chatter coming from a mobile phone. In the early morning, unless there has been a discovery in the night, the search will begin again with local help. Farm labourers will form a line to beat the undergrowth and walk the woods. They'll rove the harvest fields.

'First light,' Maidment predicts.

Zenobia waits for the water in the electric kettle to boil, emptying away what she has heated the teapot with. She makes the tea, then slices a tomato. She thought of making toast, buttering it and cutting it into fingers, but decided on a sandwich instead. It's hard to know what to prepare for someone at a quarter to twelve at night, someone who's sick with worry.

'She said she wanted nothing,' Maidment reminds her, 'and he's not back yet.' The Lindbergh ransom sum was twice as much as the twenty-five thousand, but they had it and they paid it, not knowing that their baby had already been murdered. An illiterate German immigrant the abductor was.

'She can't want nothing for ever. It could be I should sit with her.'

'She has the dog, of course.'

An hour ago he heard Mrs Iveson moving about. She went from the drawing-room to the conservatory and was settling down there with the dog when he went to ask her if she needed anything. He opened a window for her.

'I'll take the tray in. Look in yourself, why don't you, before you go upstairs? If she wants company she'll say so.'

'I couldn't go upstairs tonight.'

Maidment, who intends to retire in the usual way, refrains from arguing that rest offers strength, and takes his jacket from the back of a chair. Rhymer the name of the elderly butler who knew about the Lindberghs was, Rhymer who touched the port and suffered for it. The old man's knotted features appear in Maidment's recall, the addled look that had developed in the bloodshot eyes. Gout and worse affected him in his work and they found him early, passed away quietly in a lavatory the night before. The pantryman was next in line for the position.

'Nothing can be done but wait.' Picking up the tray, Maidment satisfies himself with the observation. The Lone Eagle they called Lindbergh after his Atlantic flight, Rhymer said. The German was a jobbing carpenter, trusted in people's houses.

'I couldn't,' Zenobia repeats, filling the kettle again for the kitchen tea. 'I couldn't lie there sleepless.'

'I'll chance it myself for a while.' For all they know, it could have been on the News, but sometimes of course the police will keep quiet for reasons of their own. Maidment pauses at the door, about to mention the News, but decides against that also.

'I brought you something, Mrs Iveson,' he says in the conservatory. He hesitates for a moment, since this is going against her wishes, neither tea nor food requested. Disturbed by his entry, the dog stands up and stretches.

'That's kind of you, Maidment.'

'It's just a little.'

'Thank you.'

She's always polite and civil. She's distant, but that's her way; getting to know her, you come to understand that. A different manner of shyness in mother and daughter; less than a week ago he remarked on that.

He clears a space for the tray and pulls the wicker table a little closer to her. She has been waiting for the telephone in the hall to ring: you can tell that from how she is.

'All we can do,' she says.

The Lindbergh family was never the same again, Rhymer said; you had money, you had trouble; they took it from you, they killed you for it. Servants to money, the well-to-do were: when it came down to it, everyone was a servant, Rhymer maintained, unaware that most of his utterances were taken with a pinch of salt.

'I can't believe it was just some woman walking by. Do you think it was, Maidment?'

'It's hard to know what to believe, Mrs Iveson.' The trouble with a woman who'd take a baby, she could be a mental case. Without a shadow of doubt, the man who climbed up to the Lindberghs' window was what they'd call a nutter nowadays.

'You never had children, Maidment?'

She surprises him, asking that, and the question coming so suddenly. There is an intimacy in the query, as if what has happened this afternoon has changed their relationship, as if formality no longer makes sense.

'No, we never did.'

With encumbrances, they wouldn't have held a position down. They'd have to have gone for a different kind of house right from the beginning. He explains this, passing the time for her because it's what she wants. Her voice is empty, but she keeps the conversation going.

'This was the work you chose? Both of you?'

'We met through the work. When the times changed we went as a couple because couples were the thing then. Zenobia picked up the kitchen knowledge, although lady's maid she'd have preferred, upstairs being what she knew. Beggars can't be choosers.'

'My daughter thought the world of you both.'

'She was the soul of kindness, your daughter.'

'I've let her down.'

'She'd be the last to say that.'

The tray is as he has placed it. She hasn't poured her tea. She stares at the prickles of a plant he considers unattractive. Ripening fast, the grapes hang all around her. It's hard to imagine, she says, that anyone wouldn't stop to think before causing such distress.

Greed takes care of that, Maidment refrains from stating. It was greed that possessed an illiterate foreigner when he hatched his plot, fear that caused him to commit his more terrible crime. When greed and fear get going, who stops to think?

'I would pay anything,' she says, and Maidment can think of no suitable rejoinder. He pours her tea for her, handing her cup and saucer. A sudden longing to have a cigarette stirs in him. The dog is restless, he says, and takes her with him to the darkened garden.

*

'Still we've never been to Scarrow Hill,' Zenobia hears herself remark, and then they're there. In the picnic area she spreads out the lunch-time fare, bread and salad, meat-loaf she made herself. Exposed on spongy hillside turf, an outline of grey rock depicts a giant.

She wakes abruptly. Around her on the kitchen table is the brass she has collected from all over the house, and Duraglit and cloths. There's the silver, too: the ornamental pheasants from the dining-room, sugar-casters, toast racks and cutlery, the silver eggs that came from Poland, the Polish crucifixes. An hour she has spent already with the Duraglit and Goddard's; before that she rearranged the tins and bottles on the cold-room shelves, and washed the passage and the cold-room floor. It's five to three now.

She blinks and rubs her eyes, dragging herself back to fuller consciousness. There was a nurse who killed babies. Four babies, maybe more. A woman pretended to be preg-nant, preparing her neighbours and her husband for what she intended to do, but when she got the baby she neglected it and it died. Other babies were taken in order to be tortured and afterwards a woman sought forgiveness, pointing out the burial places.

'You take it easy, madam,' the police officer who did the talking sought to soothe her when her voice rose anxiously in answer to a question. Strong tea, he advised; and counsel-lors were available. But prayer is Zenobia's way. As drowsiness is dispersed, she prays again.

*

'A Mrs Ferry died tonight.'

At the sound of Thaddeus's voice, Rosie lumbers to her feet, yawning and stretching herself again. The window Maidment opened earlier is closed now. In the conservatory only a single table lamp is lit.

'That was the telephone call?'

'Yes.'

He watches her nodding: she isn't interested. In the brief,

unemphatic motion of her head there is the weariness of defeat, as if time, by simply passing, has drained her of everything but this fatigue. Standing until now, Thaddeus sits down in the second wicker chair. Rosie comes to him, to rest her chin on his knees. He strokes her head.

'There's been nothing since,' she says.

'I'm sorry I went away.'

'You looked for her?'

He shakes his head. There was panic in his restlessness; he ran away from thought, but of course you can't do that. Talk is a help: in the last few moments he has discovered that. Any words, it hardly matters what they are, and the effort of releasing them: had he gone into the Old Edward, he might have stayed for ages.

'I have never been so afraid,' she says.

'Nor I, I think.'

Zenobia is with them, as suddenly and as silently as an apparition. She has heard their voices, she offers coffee, or tea again. She picks up the tray on which her sandwich has not been touched, tea poured out and left. Thaddeus says:

'You should go to bed, Zenobia.'

'I'm better up, I thought.'

When she has gone he says: 'I feel I am being punished.'

There is no response, but even so he continues.

'Mrs Ferry was a woman I ill-used. I had a peculiar childhood.' It left uneasiness behind, he says, and tells her about that. 'I have never trusted people. You were right to be doubtful: the untrusting are untrustworthy.'

'I was ungenerous. I rushed in foolishly, as if your marriage were somehow mine to order.'

'Your lack of generosity is more kindly called perception.'

'I don't think I said at lunch-time that I have come to understand why Letitia loved you.'

'I was the last of her lame ducks. There was a bargain of some kind in our marriage, in the giving and the taking. But gradually it got lost, as if all it had ever been was a means to an end. I would have given half my life then to have loved Letitia. Today it will begin, I used to think. In some random moment of the morning, or after tea, or when we've gone to bed. But it never did.'

'All that does not belong now.'

'It is something to say.'

'Why do you not blame me?'

'Blame does no good.'

Vaguely, she nods again, the same tired gesture of acknow-ledgement, not up to conversation. Thaddeus turns off the lamp on the table, and the conservatory is more softly lit by the haze of early morning. He does not want this day, so gently coming. He does not want its minutes and its hours, its afternoon and its evening, its relentless happening.

'A miracle it has seemed like,' Mrs Iveson hears him say, and is confused until he adds: 'Loving Georgina.'

*

She dreamed of Scarrow Hill, Zenobia says, and Maidment remembers from his own sleep a raw-faced bookie in a jaunty hat, and polka dots and hoops and jockeys' chat, Quick One at nines, K. McNamara up. There are, before or after that, her wedding-dress hanging on the wardrobe door, his carnation in a tumbler by the wash-basin. There was his own voice singing 'Drink To Me Only'.

'It was to say a woman died,' Zenobia passes on. 'That phone call that came earlier.'

'What woman?'

She gives the name. Bleary, he feels he's dreaming still. Not quite in the kitchen yet, but hovering in the doorway as he sometimes likes to, he averts his head to belch away a little air. Slowly he advances to the table and sits down.

'What's this then?'

'I looked in at the conservatory to see if anything was needed.'

'They're there?'

'And have been a long while.'

'So Mrs Ferry's passed on her way?'

'Dead was what I heard.'

'Mrs Ferry was the woman quarrelled over the afternoon of the accident.'

'You said.'

Each time she passed through the hall, returning the brass and silver pieces to their places, Zenobia says she heard the voices continuing in the conservatory. It not being her place to listen, she didn't do so. What she heard about the woman there'd been the quarrel over was said when she looked in to see if anything was needed.

'I dropped off a second and had that dream about the Scarrow Man.'

'I doubt my eyes closed,' Maidment touchily retorts, annoyed because it seems he might have passed the hours more profitably. He woke up and saw the other bed empty. Someone took the baby, he remembered then.

'Bloody hell!' he loudly and with suddenness exclaims.

'Jesus bloody hell!'

In astonishment, Zenobia looks across the table at him. He is not given to this. Coarseness and blasphemy have never been his way.

'We should have drawn special attention to that girl and her ring,' his explanation comes, his tone still cross. 'Out of the way, that episode was.'

'Oh, surely not.'

'Out of the way from start to finish.'

'Well, mention it when they come back. No call for rowdiness.'

'I said at the time. High and low she took him, after a ring that never saw the light of day in this house. I said it to you where you're sitting now.'

'No call for violent language neither.'

'A time like this, it's normal to speak straight out.'

His continuing vexation infects Zenobia. She responds as, years ago, she occasionally did in their circumspect marriage.

'Was it speaking straight out to mention your bones to that man? Ridiculous, that sounded.'

'What bones? What're you talking about?'

'It's meaningless when you say you'll lay down your bones. If you should have spoken about the girl and her ring, why didn't you instead of going on about your bones?'

Astonished in turn, Maidment goes quiet. He stares at the scrubbed surface of the table, the furrows in the grain. Nothing more is said.

★

At half past five, faint beads of dew on the morning cob-webs, Thaddeus crosses one lawn and then the other, Rosie trailing behind him. He gathers tools from the shed in the yard: pliers and a hammer with a claw, wire-cutters and spade. The day he made the pen for Letitia's pullets – out of sight, behind the summer-house – it took all morning. Dismantling promises to be quicker.

It was Letitia who planted the geranium banks he passes now – clumps of Lohfelden and Ridsko and Mrs Kendall Clark, Lily Lovell and Lissadell. She wanted to have a part of the garden hers and cleared spring weeds and cut down nettles and dug up docks. She made her own wild corner, and her calm presence seems fleetingly there again among the echium and poppies, a Bach cantata soft on her transistor. Surely it is enough that she has died. Thinking that, for a moment it all seems one to Thaddeus, too: the death and what so soon has followed it.

The thought still there, he patiently extracts the staples that attach the chicken-wire to the posts he drove into the grass, dropping the staples into one half of a plastic container that once held spring water. He rolls up each length of wire as it becomes free and levers the posts back and forth until they're loose enough to pull up. Only one does not come easily and he has to use the spade.

There are four coils of chicken-wire when he has finished, and eight posts which can be used for something else. The door he made of chicken-wire on a frame may be useful also. He fills the holes left in the grass with soil, ramming it home with his heel.

White sweet-pea thrives not far from where he works. Herbs are separated by narrow brick-paved paths: tarragon and apple-mint and basil, sage and parsley and rosemary and thyme, chives in profusion. A twisted trunk of wistaria is as thick as a man's thigh, its tendrils stretching for yards on either side of the archway in which, yesterday, the door was found open. It is another cloudless day.

The branches of the cherry tree that marks this corner stretch over the patch that was suitable for hens. Tidying up there, after two hours' work, Thaddeus hears the distant crunch of car tyres and pauses in his search for the short lengths of binding wire he has used, lost somewhere in the grass. Voices carry to him. A police car has returned.

The detective inspector of yesterday, whose name has registered neither in the kitchen nor the drawing-room although it was repeated in both, is less dishevelled this morning. He is wearing a different tie and a clean shirt, the trousers of his brown suit pressed overnight. His name is Baker, christened Brian Keith, but known as Dusty among his friends and colleagues.

The hall door is open when he reaches it, leaving Denise Flynn on the car phone. The hall itself is empty, but the beaky-faced houseman appears, his unobtrusive tread suggesting to a detective's trained observation a man who enjoys moving silently. Yesterday he had him down as slippery. There was a Maidment he arrested once, an unsuccessful embezzler.

'You've been informed we have a description, Mr Maidment?' Since the opportunity is there, he feels he may as well start with this man as with anyone. He repeats the description that has come in, from a railway employee and kids playing on the towpath: a girl with a bundle, in a hurry on the towpath, nervous on the railway platform, a girl of slight build, with glasses, in a T-shirt with a musical motif on it, short blue denim skirt.

'Ring a bell at all, Mr Maidment?'

Hoping to hear in response, after the usual moment of blankness, that this could possibly fit a girl of the locality, the detective hears instead that this is a girl who recently came twice to the house, the first time after a nursemaid's job that was advertised, the second in search of a ring she'd dropped.

'When was this, Mr Maidment?'

'The ring was less than a week ago.'

This is confirmed when the question is put later to the father and the grandmother, who also agree that the description fits.

'You'll have the details, sir? Name, address? She would have passed all that on?'

'Emily something, I think.'

Mrs Iveson shakes her head. Emily was the one with frizzy black hair.

Other first names are mentioned, Kylie and Dawne, but it's agreed that the girl in question was neither. No addresses or telephone numbers were retained, nor even known, none of the girls being suitable for the position.

'The girl we're talking about, would she have brought references? Would there be a name that comes back from being on a reference, sir?'

They remember a reference, passed from one to the other, then back to the girl. It hadn't impressed them.

'And the name on it, sir? Madam? Nothing at all comes back? Nothing jotted down, sir?'

'It wasn't necessary.'

'The girl returned, I understand. A ring she lost while she was here?'

'Yes.' There is a pause. 'We mentioned the girl yesterday.'

The man in the hall said the same, regretting he had not made more of this girl's return to the house.

'She just turned up, did she?'

'She telephoned beforehand to ask if we'd found her ring.'

'I understand, sir. And would she have given her name then?'

'She may have. But I think I'd remember if she had.'

It has been a shock that the abductor is known; that shows in both their faces, his drawn and exhausted, hers nervily agitated. He remains still, motionless by the bookcases; she moves about, quite different from yesterday. He apparently was puzzled at first, when the girl was on the phone, not knowing who she was, then realizing she was one of the girls they'd interviewed.

'You realized which girl particularly, sir?'

'The last one who came, she said, and I remembered.'

'I understand there have been phone calls to the house during the past few weeks. Nuisance calls.'

'Yes.'

'And you answered the phone yourself, sir, when the girl rang about her ring?'

'Yes, I did.'

'You don't recall exactly what was said, I suppose?'

'She asked if the ring had been found.'

'And of course it hadn't?'

'No.'

'She then suggested coming out here again?'

'While she was still on the phone I looked where she'd been sitting. There was nothing there.'

'Did you expect to find something, sir?'

'There seemed no reason why the ring shouldn't be there. I asked her if she could let me have a telephone number. So that we could contact her in case anything came to light.'

'But you didn't think anything would.'

'I'd no idea.'

'And what number did she give you, sir?'

She didn't give a number. If she had he would remember writing it down, and Mrs Iveson interrupts to say that none of this makes sense. Why should a girl who's hardly known to them tell lies about a ring? Why should she steal a baby?

'It's what we're endeavouring to find out, madam. We can only find out by asking questions. There is no other way.'

'We've told you what we can. We're both of us beside ourselves with worry.'

'I do appreciate that, Mrs Iveson.'

'My God, I wish you did. Thaddeus – '

'They're doing their best.'

'Thank you, sir. So the girl preferred to return in person when she might have left a number? That didn't strike you as odd, sir?'

'I assumed she wasn't on the phone. She mentioned looking for her ring on the drive, and on the lane she'd walked along. She was uncertain about where she'd dropped it. She said she was sorry for being a nuisance. The ring wasn't valuable, she said, but there was some sentimental attachment.'

'And it didn't strike you as unusual, sir, that she should want to search your drive for an object as small as a ring? A period of time had passed, after all. Cars presumably had come and gone.'

'A needle in a haystack, I thought. I think I said it.'

'Which you must have said again when she arrived out here. The same day was that?'

'No, some days later.'

'And what precisely occurred then, Mr Davenant?'

'We looked together, down the sides of the sofa. We went upstairs to the nursery.'

'Why was that, sir?'

'Because my mother-in-law had brought the girl to the nursery when she was here before.'

'And the ring was nowhere in the nursery?'

'No, it wasn't.'

'So the girl went away then?'

'She looked again in this room. She asked if she might, just to be sure.'

'And there was nothing?'

'No.'

'And then she examined the drive and the lane she had walked along? Or had she done that already?'

'I honestly don't know.'

'I don't think she was looking for anything very much after she left the house.' Mrs Iveson intervenes again, calmer now.

'You observed the girl, Mrs Iveson?'

'Yes.'

'And you were . . .?'

'I was where I was yesterday when Georgina was taken. In the shade of the catalpa tree.'

'Anything about the girl, Mrs Iveson, when you took

her up to the nursery the day she came to be interviewed?'

'Only that she wouldn't do. The day she came to look for her ring she stood on the tarmac staring at me.'

'Staring at you, Mrs Iveson?'

'Yes, I do remember that.'

'I see. And did she leave a description of this ring, sir? Just in case?'

'Soapstone, she said. Grey soapstone.'

'And this time she would have left you some means of contacting her before she went on her way, sir?'

'No, she didn't.'

'So if at some point the ring actually did surface, you still wouldn't have known what to do about it?'

'By then I really didn't believe it had been lost in the house. If it turned up anywhere else, no, we wouldn't have known what to do about it.'

'Didn't cross your mind, sir, that for some reason this girl was making the whole thing up?'

'No, it didn't.'

Detective Inspector Baker – known for his doggedness in the force, recently promoted after eleven successful years in the vice squad – considers it extraordinary that a would-be employee came to this house, was interviewed for a position, answered questions as to suitability and background, and walked away again without a note being kept of her name. That she later telephoned with a story a child wouldn't have fallen for, and ended up being assisted to search for a non-existent item of jewellery beggars all reasonable belief. In a brief wave of nostalgia, the inspector recalls the quick-witted pornographers and street pimps whose prevarications and deceptions were so often and so precisely presented to him. There is a measured helpfulness about the man he has been questioning, a clear determination not to become emotional. The old lady's in shock and can't, of course, be blamed.

'Well, there seems no doubt that it was this girl.' He nods at both of them, but when he is asked if the establishing of this identification is going to make the search for the baby easier, he adopts the stony-faced reticence of detectives in films, hoping to conceal the fact that he doesn't know. The girl was confident. She walked into a garden and took a sleeping baby, in full view of anyone who might have been at a window. Without a shadow of a doubt, she had previously established the lie of the land and the routine of the household, had clearly waited until the dog was out of the way; and having successfully collected the baby, took the path through the fields and then by the canal in order to avoid being seen on the lanes or waiting for a bus. She'd timed the whole thing so that she could slip on to the four twenty-three, which yesterday had run only two and a half minutes late. The confident ones are often the most dangerous.

'She was normal, would you say, sir? From your observation when she returned that day?'

'Normal?'

'Manner and that. Her behaviour odd or peculiar in any way?'

'She talked rather a lot, I remember.'

'You can't remember what about, I suppose?'

'To tell the truth, I didn't really listen.'

'Spoke about the baby, did she?'

'I don't think so. More about herself. There was something to do with a mother in Australia.'

'Ah. And nothing else comes back, I suppose?'

'She said that she'd put flowers on my wife's grave.'

'My God!' Mrs Iveson's invocation is an anguished mutter, which seems to the detective aptly to sum up this whole extraordinary affair.

'And do you think she did, sir?'

'I don't know.'

'You didn't think the girl was on anything, sir?'

'Drugs, you mean?'

'They sometimes are.'

'She could have been. That didn't occur to me.'

'No reason why it should have, of course. With someone who was a stranger to you.'

There is a silent moment, incidentally there when the questioning ceases. The girl has taken her chance, the detective muses, attracted by the baby she saw when first she was shown the nursery. It could be something misheard, that she placed flowers on the grave of a woman she never knew. Most likely it is that, he speculates, but does not say so.

★

The local search that Maidment predicted is not carried out: the immediate locality is of less interest now. Again, for hours, the telephone does not ring. All morning there is silence. No breakfast is taken, no lunch. It is the afternoon of the day Thaddeus has dreaded when the news comes, preceding WPC Denise Flynn, who later carries the stolen baby from the police car to the house.

★

'A shut-up building,' Maidment says, 'that used to be a home for unwanted children. A lad poking round found her.'

Aghast, Zenobia turns from the sink, a potato half scraped in her hand. She is hungry, and so must everyone else be. She has made sandwiches for the police who have returned yet again, feeling that they, too, are probably in need of food. The kitchen quarrel which brought a coolness in the night seems to belong to some distant time, and plays no part now.

'Was the girl . . . ,' she begins to ask, intending to inquire if the girl responsible for the stealing was frightened off by the lad poking round, or has been found and apprehended. In fact, with the three words hanging, she is answered without addition to them.

'No one else was there but the baby, with food laid out on the floor, not that it was of use to her. As far as can be ascertained, the next thing was she got carried by this lad through the streets, to the quarters of the Salvation Army.'

Zenobia does not entirely follow this, wondering where the Salvation Army comes into it. She does not speak, knowing it is unnecessary, since her confusion is apparent in her face.

'The lad shouldn't have been in a house due for demolition, but there's no fuss made about that. A few marbles short, by all accounts, but no one's on about that either.'

'He couldn't be – ?'

'We know who took her, dear.'

Never in all his years in other people's houses has Maidment garnered so much or so richly in so brief a time. The disappointment of missing the news of Mrs Ferry's death when it came is amply compensated. Pleasure flushes his edgy features, lights his eyes, causes a mild quivering of his lips when he reports what he has to. Observing these signs of his excitement, Zenobia is concerned for him; but her concern is slight, for the relief she experienced when the child was found continues so joyfully to possess her that all other emotions fall back. And what does it matter how the crime was committed, or even by whom, now that the thing is over? Private by her bedside, she has already knelt in gratitude.

'Sugar lumps for the dog.' She hears her husband repeat what he has stated several times already. 'Chocolate or mixed sweets, a burglar's ploy. Loitering with intent under four pairs of eyes.'

He extracts a packet of cigarettes and a lighter from a pocket, and for an alarming moment it seems to Zenobia that he may light up in the kitchen, which he hasn't done since their first position as a couple, the morning they came down to discover the water tanks had overflowed in the night.

'Didn't I say I didn't like the look of her,' he's saying now, 'the time she came back with her story?'

With the cigarettes and lighter still safely in his palm, he moves towards the passage that leads to the yard. In the doorway he selects a cigarette and returns the packet to his pocket. Left to him, he says, he wouldn't have let her in that day.

Zenobia has little memory of the girl who is suspected, having glanced only once in her direction that afternoon, when the landing curtains needed a stitch. She looked an unremarkable girl as far as Zenobia can remember, small and peering a bit, the way a short-sighted girl might, nothing special. It all just goes to show, Zenobia's view is, and silently she gives thanks again.

14

The ordeal, which has lasted a little longer than twenty-three hours, has left with Mrs Iveson what she knows will always be there: Maidment white-faced in the sunshine when she asked him to look among the shrubs, the trembling of his hands when he returned; Thaddeus saying blame does no good; Zenobia confessing later that some time in that night she gave up hope.

We are left with no explanation and no sign of one, she writes the news to Sussex. *Why any of it happened is the mystery we must live with, for I do not believe they will find the girl. If that boy had not gone to the place when he did Georgina would not be alive. That that was what the girl intended we must live with, too.*

She does not think, she adds, that she can remain at Quincunx House. She shall, of course, until a new arrangement is made, but in the end the arrangement she suggested herself has been shown to be a failure. *Thaddeus, though, does not accept my view and is adamant it were better I stayed. I press him – not that I want to go, but feel I should – and still he does not see it. So it is left. Stubbornness is a quality I have not noticed in him before.*

The only flowers Thaddeus has ever sent Mrs Ferry he sends on the day the letter that tells of this unresolved consequence is posted. Having forgotten about the funeral, he remembers the night before it is to take place and telephones first thing, relieved to find he is not too late. Cut flowers, not a wreath, he stipulates, bright colours, the brightest mixed together. When the time comes for the woman he was once attracted by to lie briefly in the crematorium chapel he thinks of her. 'A generous spirit,' he does not know the clergyman's description is, but guesses that a favourite tune is played and that the chef who was at the Beech Trees is there. A few others are present too, her onetime husband arriving five minutes late, delayed by traffic on his journey down from Lytham St Annes, his second wife waiting in the car, feeling that to be proper in the circumstances.

The week that brought Mrs Ferry's death and the ordeal of Georgina's abduction comes to an end, and on the Sunday that finishes it Mrs Iveson agrees to think further about her decision, and next morning agrees to stay. The days settle back into ordinariness then, as the summer heatwave continues. From Sussex come commiserations and exclamations of outrage in a shaky hand. Terrible things happen, it is declared; that is life today, enlightened times or not. A postscript adds that the cataract operation, twice postponed, is to take place at last, next month. And news goes back to Sussex of Georgina's teething.

In time, the first green specks of Thaddeus's winter parsley appear. *Murder in Mock Street* is taken from the drawing-room shelves, and then *The Corpse on the Fourteenth Green*. 'My!' Zenobia marvels on a weekend outing to Scarrow Hill, for the giant is taller than in her dream, and shocking in a way she failed to anticipate. Maidment wins with Cappoquin Boy. No change is reported from St Bee's.

Of course, we live in fear, Mrs Iveson brings herself to confess, *that again we are watched, that even now she comes by night to the garden, that again she will hurt us. I see her face, staring at me from where she stood that day, the sunlight glinting on her glasses.*

But no one comes to the garden in the way Mrs Iveson dreads, either by night or by day. Instead there are the first late-August signs of autumn there, a softness in the fading colours.

15

A man exercises greyhounds on the towpath where horses once drew the narrow boats of the canal. The muddy sediment that separates the two banks is dankly shadowed, its surface active with autumn insects. The greyhounds are obedient, running on and turning when they're whistled back, one jet black, the other speckled.

The walk from the town has taken Albert forty-seven minutes, the time checked on his Zenith because he likes to check the passing of time. He has paused quite often to watch the greyhounds racing on the towpath opposite; now, he turns to the right, leaving them behind when he sees the spire of the church in the distance, and houses clustered nearer. A few minutes later the notice he has been told about says the petrol pump is out of order. Then there is the shop, and the public house next door to it. 'That name's all over the graveyard,' she said, and there it is: *Davenant* on upright and horizontal stones. 'Thaddeus Davenant,' she said, but there's no one answering to that, Johns and Williams and Percivals mostly, all sorts when it comes to the women. No stone yet marks the newest grave; she said that, too.

He leaves the graveyard, and on the lane a tractor comes slowly towards him and he stands in against the hedge to let it pass. The driver waves his thanks, an old man in a cap, his glance passing inquisitively over Albert's clothing – the red and blue uniform he has coveted for so long, found for him when he was accepted into the ranks.

It's quiet in the lane once the tractor noise has faded, no aeroplanes to look up at, no one about. The edges of the leaves are withering; there are a few white flowers, a few pink and yellow, in among the brambles. The sky is grey and dull, all sunshine gone, but Albert doesn't mind: there are the flowers, even though they're past their best. 'Immortal, Invisible' is the hymn that is in his mind. He has never walked in the country before.

There's a wood behind a fence of barbed wire. Some sort of path through fields he was told about, but he doesn't look for it. A breeze is getting up, rippling through a crop and in the high grass of a meadow. Merle said she came from the country, a big house by a river, brown horses grazing, like in the picture above Mr Hoates's desk. Don't ever throw down sweet papers in a country field, Miss Rapp ruled. Because the country was our heritage.

Drops of rain begin, heavy drops that spread damp patches on Albert's jacket and are cold on his forehead and his cheeks. Cows move slowly in a field, all going together, maybe for shelter. The gateless pillars that have been described are straight ahead. The drops have become a downfall, puddles already filling, the surface of the lane awash.

On the drive, the parched laurels drip and glisten; water streams into gratings; Albert's shoes are soaked. He blinks the rain out of his eyes, he turns up the collar of his jacket. It is the first time rain has fallen on his uniform. Who'd ever have thought that it could rain?

★

'A look of an egg about the face,' Maidment reports. 'With

eyes that do not express a lot, if anything at all. Drenched from head to foot. I wonder he didn't shelter.' He leaves the best till last. 'Togged out by the Salvation Army.'

'Why's that?'

'I'm telling you what's there.'

'You know when the Salvation Army was mentioned.'

This has struck Maidment too. A Salvation Army barracks, or whatever the term is. The name of the street was given, but he has forgotten.

'He say what he wanted?'

'A word. He said he wanted a word. He called me sir.'

'It'll be that boy.'

Weeks have passed since their outing to Scarrow Hill. On subsequent Sundays there have been visits to Notham Manor and the Dolls' Museum at Hindesleigh, to Tattermarle Castle and a steam-engine display in a field. On each occasion Zenobia has attended church *en route* while Maidment read the *News of the World* in the Subaru. 'No, I want to forget about it,' Zenobia has firmly laid down when attempts have been made by her husband to embark on fresh speculation about the abduction. She doesn't at all like the advent of this boy.

'Come for another handout.' And Maidment pronounces fiscal gain to be the universal language of the age, cure for all ills, salver of all conscience.

'You'll need to take in tea,' Zenobia interrupts this flow, lifting a cherry cake from a tin. 'You have tobacco on your breath,' she points out also. 'Take Listerine, I would.'

★

'You ever get the planes going over?' Albert asks. 'Alitalia? Icelandic? Air Canada with the leaf? Air India, you get?'

Nothing much in the way of plane traffic, they say, the man saying it first. 'Mrs Iveson,' she said when he came into the room and he wondered how she was spelling that, but didn't ask. 'Mr Davenant,' she said, and he didn't say he knew.

Virgin has the pin-up, he says, the Saudis have the swords, the Irish the shamrock. 'You'd know a shamrock never grew in England, sir?'

The man Pettie took the shine to nods. The woman she didn't like says the shamrock is special to St Patrick, which he had ready to say himself. Pettie got off on the wrong foot with her on account she gave short on the fares, but it could have been she didn't mean to. It could have been she hadn't checked it out. He didn't say it to Pettie, a waste of breath that would have been. Pettie didn't go for her and that was that.

'He took it as a sign.' He explains in case there is confusion about the shamrock. 'A three-leaved clover.'

'Yes, he did.'

'You'd know it's a bird on a lot of them, sir? One way or another, not that people realize. Singapore for starters, sir. Then again Indonesia. Then again Nigeria and the Germans.'

'I see.'

'Not much to Cathay Pacific, sir. Not much to Egypt Air.'

'No, I suppose not.'

'They give me the money, sir. What you sent.'

They nod their heads. A Friday it was when she came out here the first time, a Saturday a.m. when she said Thaddeus Davenant the first time in the Soft Rock.

'We're extremely grateful to you,' the woman says.

'They said you was grateful.'

'More than we can express.'

The man who opened the door comes in with a tray. It's laden down with a cake and toast cut into strips, and a plate of biscuits, and jam, and plates and cups and saucers. You can tell there's butter on the toast from the glisten.

'Georgina Belle recovered from her adventure?' He planned to say that first of all, but he forgot, so he says it now. Then he asks about Iveson, how it's spelt, explaining that he takes an interest in a name.

'I, v, e,' the woman says, 's, o, n.'

The man puts the tray down. He fiddles with the cups and saucers, setting them out. Pettie didn't go for him, either. She didn't like the way he looked at her when he opened the front door. You wouldn't trust a man like that, she said.

'Iveson,' the woman repeats, and he's put in mind of Ivy On Her Own, who sang for Leeroy. Still not speaking, the man who brought the tray in goes away.

'Why d'you call her that?' the woman asks. 'Georgina Belle?'

'The baby that is, Mrs Iveson.'

'Just Georgina it is.'

He mentions Leeroy. Ivy On Her Own, he explains, Bob Iron and the Metalmen. 'I thought it was Georgina Belle,' he says, and explains that Leeroy's singers didn't exist, that no one could hear them except Leeroy. Probably no one can to this day, he explains.

'I see,' the woman says.

'One of those things, like.'

He likes the cup his tea's in, flowers all over it and a gold ring on the edge, and another round the saucer. He likes the cake he's eating, as good as anything Mr Kipling does. 'You know Mr Kipling at all?' he asks them and then he realizes they think he means personally so he explains that Mr Kipling is a cake-maker. Mrs Biddle is partial to Mr Kipling's almond slices, he says, anything with jam in it and Mrs Biddle's away. When she was younger she had to watch her waist.

'All right then, Mrs Iveson?'

'Yes, of course.'

'Not that Mrs Biddle's stout these days. Skin and bone, as a matter of fact.'

'Would you like to see Georgina? I'm sure you would.'

She goes away and Thaddeus Davenant offers him the biscuits. The dog's asleep, stretched out in a corner. There are more books in those bookcases than he has ever seen in a living-room before. Albert says that, keeping things going.

'What's his name, sir?' he inquires, looking over at the dog.

'Rosie.'

He remembers. And he remembers this same dog described, friendly and brown, and how he warned her that you can't be too careful with a dog. The rain's still coming down, sounding on the window glass.

'They don't like a uniform, sir. Depending on the dog, a postman said to me once.'

'Postmen have a lot to put up with in that respect.'

He's a man who doesn't say much, which maybe was what she took to. She could sit in silence with a person, it didn't matter. When they lived in the glasshouse she didn't speak herself for hours on end. It would come on dark and he daren't flash on his torch, but she never minded. She'd things to think about, she said.

'You read all them books, sir?'

'Not all of them. But most, I think, one way or another.'

Mrs Biddle has a few behind glass in the hall. Not his business, so he never took one out. Magazines are more Mrs Biddle's thing. *Hello!* and *Chic* he gets her, the *People's Friend*.

'Read a Book with Me, by the Man Who Sees. You come across that, sir? I come across it somewhere, maybe Miss Rapp it was. The *Home Encyclopaedia* we had. *Arthur Mee's Talks for Boys*, sir? You'd have known that in your young days?'

'No. No, I'm afraid I didn't.'

'You ever go on Varig, Mr Davenant? Varig Brazilian?'

'Actually, I've never flown.'

'They have the rainforest down Brazil way.'

'Yes, they do.'

Mrs Iveson is back with the baby, and the baby's eyes are fixed on him, not that she shows recognition. Too much to expect, in a baby.

'Hullo, there,' he says.

She puts the baby down on a chair, bunching it back into a corner, with a cushion in front of it in case it tumbles off, although it's hard to see how it could.

'Is it Albert?' she asks. 'I think at the time they said Albert.'

'What?'

'Did you tell us your name?'

He feels foolish, as he did when he forgot about the dog being mentioned. He should have given his name when he entered the room. Best to call it an adventure was what he was concentrating on, best to smile, which he did, only he forgot to give his name.

'Albert Luffe.'

'We guessed when we saw your uniform. We were told you took Georgina to one of your hostels.'

'You think it's all right?' He strokes one lapel and then the other, to indicate what he means. They say it suits him. 'You look ridiculous, dear,' Mrs Biddle said the first time he wore it, taking against it because it was something new. 'You're in that uniform again,' she has taken to calling out, knowing he has it on when he doesn't look in to say goodbye to her on his way out. Mrs Biddle needn't see it if she doesn't want to, no way he'd foist something new on her. He didn't tell her Captain Evans is going to teach him an instrument, soon as they find out which one he'd be all right on. Best not to bring it up if it isn't what she wants.

'Sorry about that, Mrs Iveson.'

'Sorry?'

'I had it in mind to give my name first thing. Otherwise you'd be confused.'

'It doesn't matter in the least.'

'I wasn't wearing my uniform that day, as a matter of fact. I wasn't in the Army even. To tell you the truth, I wouldn't be in the Army if it wasn't for that day.'

She smiles at him. She says they owe the baby's life to his quick thinking, knowing what to do.

'No sweat, Mrs Iveson.'

The rain has soaked through a place in his jacket and through his trousers at the knees. He feels the dampness, colder now than a moment ago. When he gets back he'll iron the uniform first thing in case there's damage done. It was definitely Miss Rapp who was on about the Man Who Sees, some different magazine because *Hello!* and *Chic* weren't going then.

'She wasn't kicking up a row, nothing like that. Only gurgling a bit. Many's the time we had a baby left there. In the coke shed. By the doors. Many's the time we'd hear the screeching first thing, wake you up it would. Newborn, maybe a day, maybe a week. "What'll we call it?" Mrs Hoates would say.'

The other man comes back with water for the tea. He lifts the teapot lid and pours some in. He checks the food, making sure there's enough. He still doesn't speak. They take no notice of him.

Mrs Hoates would say what'll we call it, but every time she'd pick the name herself. You'd make a suggestion and she'd say lovely, but then she'd go for something else. He explains that to them, thinking he'd better, in case of misleading.

'What's this?' She smiles at him. 'What's this about, Albert?'

'The Morning Star, Mrs Iveson.'

'I think it's where he found Georgina,' Thaddeus Davenant says. 'A derelict children's home, they said.'

Albert stirs two lumps of sugar into a fresh cup of tea. The biscuits are mixed creams and chocolate-coated. He takes one that has raspberry jam in with the cream. Another thing is, it was Miss Rapp who gave the information about the shamrock, how the slave boy banished the toads and serpents, bringing in the harmless weed instead.

'Spaxton Street,' he says. 'Round the Tipp Street corner is where the brown yard doors are. You know the neighbourhood, sir? Fulcrum Street?'

'I'm afraid I don't.'

'You were a child in the home yourself, Albert?'

He says he was. He gives some other names because they're interested. He tells the story of Joey Ells, the Sunday when it snowed. Crippled, he says, and she asks about the tank, and he explains that Joey Ells thought there were steps where there weren't. An iron ladder there used to be, only it gave way under rust.

'What a terrible thing!'

You can see they both think it was terrible, and he tells how Miss Rapp walked away from the Morning Star the next day. He mentions Joe Minching and Mrs Cavey. Mrs Cavey did the cooking, he explains. The milkman sometimes stopped to play football in the yard, clattering down his crate of bottles as a goalpost.

'Your home?' she wants to know. 'You still think of it as home, Albert?'

'I have a room with Mrs Biddle these days. Appian Terrace. You know Appian Terrace, sir?'

'No, I don't think I do.'

He says where Appian Terrace is and how he came to get the room there. He says that Mrs Biddle is bed-bound, how he's worried about the teapot because the stuff is unravelling off the handle, how she could have a fall. He puts down Cat Scat because a cat comes that's a nuisance to her. But it isn't any good.

'Mrs Biddle has her memories,' he says. 'Theatrical.'

He can see the photograph Pettie was on about, the

plain dress with the collar up a bit, the woman who's in the grave they haven't erected a stone for. There was an accident once on the April outing, a red car squeezed shapeless, hub-caps and metal on the road, the radio still playing, no chance. That comes into Albert's mind, but he doesn't mention it. Too much speed, Joe Minching said, and they got out of the minibus at a Services and watched the speed, everything going by below them on the motorway, reds and greens and blues. 'More blues,' Ram said, and Leeroy argued.

He's offered the biscuits again and takes another, the chocolate heart. He tells them about the Underground because she asks if he has work. He remembers Pettie saying you could hardly see the make-up on her face and he can hardly see it today either. Mrs Biddle puts lipstick on first thing, then her powder.

'Little Mister's with the rent boys,' he says, and he watches a sadness coming into her face. He likes her clothes and the way she stands so straight when she's on her feet, and the softness in her eyes. He liked her the minute she held her hand out to him, smiling then too, giving her name. He tells about Little Mister left on the step and how he got to be called that. He tells them he heard from Merle one time that Mr and Mrs Hoates were down Portsmouth way now.

'Running an old folks' residential.'

She asks about Merle, and he says she's not around these days, not since she went up Wharfdale. Nor Bev, he says.

★

Darkened by the rainfall, the drawing-room is invaded by other people and another place, by the faces of children, black and white and Indian; by dank downstairs passages, Cardinal polish on concrete floors, a mangle forgotten in a corner; by window-panes painted white, bare stairway treads, rust marks on mattresses. A handbell rings, there is the rush of footsteps.

They listen because there is a debt they can never repay, neither by the money that has been given already nor by their attention, yet their attention continues. From time to time they do not easily follow what they're being told, bewildered by new names when they occur, the order of events a muddle. Easing ten minutes ago, the rain comes heavily again.

'Her party dress she always wore on a Sunday. The others wouldn't bother.'

His friend would put on Mrs Hoates's perfume. As soon as she saw Mrs Hoates setting off on a Sunday afternoon to visit her relation who wasn't well she would try out a different perfume. Nail-varnish she tried out once, and another time a pair of earrings. She'd do her hair in Mrs Hoates's mirror and then she'd go downstairs. There'd be the uncles' coats hanging on the hallstand pegs, the uncle with the birthmark waiting, never impatient, reading any leaflets that were lying about the hall.

'Uncles?'

' "Don't take no presents," I'd always say, but they'd take them and then they'd try to get away. You get the picture, sir?'

'Yes, we do.'

Removing a roller-blind in the hall in order to adjust the tension, Maidment gets the picture also. A hell is the picture Mrs Iveson gets, doors closed and silence, the hiding after they tried to get away. In her party dress, only one of them never minded. Pertly, she smiled at her Sunday uncle, scented and made-up for him.

'So you went back to that place all this time later and found Georgina?'

'Nothing doing in the yard, like, so I go in by the bottom window. Not a sound, Mrs Iveson. Nothing there, is what I says at first.'

Thaddeus wishes he didn't have to hear. He tries not to, apprehensive about what may be said next. He tries not to see the bleak, empty house to which his child was taken, to be abandoned for a reason that is unknown.

'I come to the bathroom, not that you'd know it with the bath gone and the basin taken down. Mrs Hoates's bathroom that was, Hoates's too. First thing I notice is the baby in a corner. I had the torch. With the windows boarded it's dark enough in there. Not that there hasn't been squatters, not that they hasn't taken a board or two down. Only you need the torch in case.'

'Of course.' Uneasy too, Mrs Iveson nods.

'No place for a baby, and I give it in at Tipp Street. I just give in Georgina Belle. I didn't tell a lie, sir.'

Thaddeus watches the shaking of the tidy head, slowly, emphatically, back and forth, back and forth, as rhythmic as a pendulum. It's not a lie when you don't say. It's not a lie when you just give something in.

'Of course it isn't,' Mrs Iveson reassures, not understanding.

Five minutes later Zenobia learns that this boy knew what he was looking for when he went to that bathroom. Well known to him and given to crime, the bespectacled girl had come to the house where he lived and had knocked on the kitchen window. She was a girl who'd vandalized a man's possessions once, who walked out on employers whenever she felt like it. Calm as you please, she told the boy she'd stolen a baby, and told him where she'd put it.

★

'She says would I hand it in. Like I done, Mrs Iveson.'

They don't say anything. Albert watches the baby trying to join her fingers together, holding them up in front of her face. She pulls them apart again. She's gurgling and smiling, trying to laugh, only she can't laugh properly, the age she is.

'She put Georgina Belle down in the Morning Star on account of everything going wrong.'

'What went wrong?' They both say that, one after the other. She says it twice.

'Pettie's plans, like.' Albert shakes his head. 'Pettie didn't know what to do.'

'Why did she take Georgina?' She says Pettie was a girl they didn't know. She came to the house by chance, she says. 'Was she hoping to get money? Did she just want a baby?'

'Mrs Biddle says Pettie's a tearaway, Mrs Iveson.'

'You should have told all this to the police.'

'Pettie took a shine to Mr Davenant, like. Pettie takes a shine to the older man, sir.'

He explains that a man showed Pettie vinyls for the floor, different colour runs and weights, what was suitable for a kitchen, what was not. Eric he was called, she saw it on his suit lapel. He lived out Wimbledon way; he took his holidays for the tennis, always got good weather. A year ago it was; every day she went on about it in the Soft Rock. And there was a fisherman once, and another time a man who took her back to his room and she was frightened when he got up to things. The older man, Albert says again, in case there is confusion.

'She took Georgina because Georgina is Mr Davenant's child? Is that it? Did she tell you what she intended?'

'Pettie was in a state, Mrs Iveson.' She wouldn't have left the Dowlers if she hadn't got into a state, and he tells them about going round to the Dowlers and Mrs Dowler shouting down the stairs. 'I never seen her in such a state as this time, Mrs Iveson, and the next thing is she takes the baby. Pettie never done that before. Like I say, I'm in the kitchen and there's this rapping on the panes. Four times she's come round only I'm on the night work and then I have a sleep.'

'You've told us all that.'

'Soon's I flashed the torch in the bathroom I saw the butterfly. Pettie'd make butterflies out of a cigarette wrapping. Then again the packet and the butts she left. Pettie'd always break a butt open. In the Soft Rock, anywhere. I flashed the torch and saw the bread and that. There could be rats, the bread'd bring rats. I was remarking that to myself when I picked up Georgina Belle.'

'Her name's Georgina.' There is a whiteness in her face, in her cheeks and around her eyes. A moment ago she kept looking at him, but now the only movement's a frown coming and going in her forehead. Her voice has changed, a crossness in it now, and the dog pokes up its head, then flops it down again. The baby has gone to sleep.

'One p.m. it was when I seen her; three-quarters of a minute past. I looked at the Zenith in case they'd ask me.'

He gave the time as three-quarters of a minute past one when they did, and they asked how he knew and he said. 'How about a tea?' Captain Evans offered him when the police left, the first time he knew Captain Evans, not even knowing his name then. All the time the butterfly and the cigarette butts and the empty cigarette packet were in his pocket because there hadn't been a chance to drop them into a bin.

'Not that Pettie'd care,' he says. 'The way she was then, she couldn't care less.'

'That girl took a baby to a house where her crying couldn't be heard. She walked away and left her.'

Everything is different in the room now. The sympathy's gone, there are no smiles. It would be all right, he thought when they said they were grateful, and when she asked if he took sugar and put the lumps in with a tongs. A clock strikes quietly in the hall, and then she says he must go immediately to the police, that he must give them Pettie's name.

'It was Pettie wore the party dress, Mrs Iveson.'

She takes no notice, nor does he. He thought they would. He thinks maybe they didn't hear, but he doesn't say it again. She says does he realize this could happen to someone else?

'Other people will suffer as we have.'

'Pettie never took babies before, Mrs Iveson. She didn't do no harm to Georgina Belle.'

She would have married the floors man. His hands were

well kept, tapering fingers, she said, the tips light on the vinyl samples. She hung about the tennis when the time for the next championships came. She'd have given him a family, she said, if that was what he wanted. She'd have cooked and mended for him.

'The baby's back safe, Mrs Iveson.'

The damp has spread, through to his shoulders and his back. There's a mark on the rug at his feet where water has dripped from the ends of his trousers, or from the jacket cuffs, he doesn't know which. She was in a state when she lost track of that Eric, same's she was when she went round to that uncle's house. The face went with the name, she said in the Soft Rock that Saturday morning, the pale eyes, no wasted flesh. Another time in the Soft Rock she put the same thing to the red-haired proprietor, not that she ever liked him. 'You hear that name?' she said. 'Thaddeus?' And winding Pettie up, the red-haired man said Thaddeus was the name of the inventor of the bikini.

'Why'd she do it?' Thaddeus Davenant is standing by the windows and he speaks with his back turned, still looking out at the rain. His voice isn't raised like hers is, but low and ordinary, as if he's not fussed, but Albert can tell he is. 'Why'd she do it?' he asks.

'Like I say, sir – '

'Why'd she take Georgina?'

'On account she was her own worst enemy, Mr Davenant. I never knew anyone more her own worst enemy.'

The baby whimpers in her sleep, a single whimper and then a sigh. She whimpered when he picked her up from the floor; she whimpered a bit on the way downstairs, maybe not liking the dark although he had the torch going.

When she wasn't much older than that, the mongol girl cried every time she woke up and it was dark. Merle walked in her sleep, Leeroy used to shout out.

'Why'd she take Georgina?' He turns round from the window to ask that again. 'Why?'

'On account it was no good, coming back here for the ring, sir.'

He didn't tell Mrs Biddle about the ring. He didn't say about the baby. A lie is a lie if it has intention was the way Miss Rapp put it. No way just saying nothing is a lie. No way it could be.

'Why was it no good?'

'Like you wouldn't have nothing to do with her, sir. She took a shine to you, Mr Davenant – '

'Yes, we know.'

'Then again, Pettie thought she'd get the minding job.'

'She wasn't suitable.'

'She thought you was offering it to her on the phone, sir. The time she called up she thought it was going to be all right from what you said, sir. Then again, the ten pounds wasn't right.'

'What ten pounds?'

'Ten eighty the cost of the fares is.'

Again nothing is said. He watches the man Pettie had a passion for turn his back again, the rain streaming on the glass of the windows. The old lady gets up and crosses to where the baby's still asleep, and then sits down in a different armchair, as still and straight as before.

'If the train fare I gave her wasn't enough she should have said so.'

'Like I say, the baby's back, Mrs Iveson – '

'Why have you come here?' Thaddeus Davenant is standing by him now, his voice still quiet. 'What do you want with us?'

'I come to tell you about Pettie, sir. So's you wouldn't think too badly of her, sir.'

'Too badly?' she says. 'What on earth do you mean?'

'Pettie was improving herself, Mrs Iveson. All the time at the Morning Star, all the time she was at the Dowlers'. She could have come down the platforms, she could have got clearing-up in the parks a few months back. She went in for the baby-minding because it was a better type of work.' Pettie was a law unto herself, he explains. 'I'd worry about Pettie, Mrs Iveson. I'd worry in the Soft Rock, times she didn't turn up.' He explains about Wharfdale, and Pettie taking lifts in a lorry. 'Pettie come out here the first time and she was on about it in the café, the picture there was on the floor, the dog coming in through them windows. I said to leave it.'

'Your friend stole a sleeping baby and left it where it could have been eaten by rats.'

'I got there quickly as I could, Mrs Iveson. Soon's ever Pettie told me. Mrs Biddle'd make the tea, she'd trip over with that teapot, but I had to take the chance. I didn't do another thing soon's Pettie told me. I said it to Captain Evans, but he reckoned Mrs Biddle'd be all right. I had to wait there for the police, the problem was.'

'She put flowers on my daughter's grave. Why'd she do that? Why'd she come looking for a ring that didn't exist? We don't understand what all this is about. We don't understand why she took against us when all we ever did was not to give her enough money for a train fare.'

'Pettie seen the photograph when she come out here, Mrs Iveson. She seen Mr Davenant grieving, she said that in the Soft Rock. Pettie took a shine to Mr Davenant, Mrs Iveson – '

'Oh, for God's sake, stop saying that!' She is furious now, her voice raised, two specks of red in her cheeks.

'It's upsetting for us.' Thaddeus Davenant is still quiet, the same as all the time he has been, hardly a change from when he was talking about the planes. 'We're grateful to you, but all this is too much for us.'

'All Pettie was doing, sir, was putting it to you the baby could be taken. Like Mrs Iveson was sitting out in the sun and the next thing she drops off. Pettie had it worked out, like Mrs Iveson would pack her bags soon's the baby went missing. You get that, sir?'

'Yes.'

'Pettie had it in mind she'd say she came back after her ring and seen a woman with the baby. She had it in mind that she manages to get the baby off the woman in the toilets.'

'I see.'

'Only the kids was playing on the towpath. Soon's the kids seen Pettie it has to be there wasn't no woman on account Pettie has the baby. Soon's – '

'Yes, we understand.'

'I come out to explain, sir, Pettie didn't mean no harm. Time of the ring was like when she went to look out for the man at the tennis championships. Miss Rapp said Pettie never meant no harm.'

'Oh, do spare us Miss Rapp!' She's furious again. She calls what he's saying a rigmarole. They don't want to hear about Miss Rapp, she says, or Mrs Biddle or Captain Evans or some man selling vinyl. It was absurd that the girl should have imagined she could be employed here. 'We're not concerned with these people. What we're concerned about is that this girl is unstable and should be put where she can't cause distress like this again.'

'Pettie's dead, Mrs Iveson.'

★

A watery sunlight has begun to brighten the room, dappling the polished oak of the floor, a single beam falling across the bookcases. Outside, a blackbird tentatively begins its warble. Thaddeus has not witnessed his mother-in-law's anger before. Replacing at last the hall's rewound blind, Maidment has not either.

Mrs Iveson herself, startled by what has just been said, senses an inner reprimand, even though her anger is still potent. The boy looks at her foolishly, his dark hair wet, his ill-fitting uniform seeming as ridiculous as the woman he spoke of said, his face gone empty, registering nothing.

No more than fifteen or so, Thaddeus remembers thinking, that girl in her grubby yellow jacket before she took it off on the afternoon of the interview. Her skirt rose up when she sat on the sofa, and she didn't pull it down. 'You've had a journey for nothing,' he said the second time she came, and she said no, not for nothing. In the nursery, when she stood so close to him, he knew and didn't want to know, darkening a truth that came from outside his life, hurrying on, away from it.

'Dead?' he says, in confusion, unable to suppress the thought that death surely does not beget death, as it seems to have this summer.

'They bulldozed down the Morning Star, sir. I saw her in the brick and stuff lifted away. I saw Pettie in the sky.'

★

Rubble swung across the sky in its great metal bucket is brought to Zenobia, and Maidment sits down at the kitchen table, upset. Nausea spreads in his stomach, where drama at a remove brings usually a ripple of pleasure.

Would she not have known what was happening? Zenobia's question is. A house knocked down around her? Would she not have heard the noise?

And Maidment says that's just it.

★

He has to say again that Pettie took a shine, but this time it's all right. It was all to do with that, he has to say.

'I could have put them in the picture if they asked me, the day they was knocking down the Morning Star. I could have told them why she done it, sir, why Pettie didn't walk away. Only I didn't hang about. No point, sir.'

'No.'

'She goes back to the Morning Star, the time she's frightened, the time the police is out looking for her.'

They've gone quiet. She's staring out into the dampness. He didn't mention it to Mrs Biddle, he says. Age she is, best not to, stuff like that. They still don't say anything, so he stands up.

The doors are opened for him – the door of the room, the outside door. On the steps they shake his hand. He says again why he came out, in case there's any confusion left. They say they understand.

He walks slowly because there is nothing to hurry for. The rain has taken away the stifling warmth, the hedgerows on either side of him drip. A breeze occasionally shakes more drops from the leaves of trees, and sometimes a withered leaf falls too.

The hymn starts in his head. He wonders what it means, *All laud we would render*. Not that it matters. Best part of the day it was, the morning hymn. *Thus provided, pardoned, guided*. Then again *Speak through the earthquake, wind and fire*. He should have told them he'll buy an instrument with the money. People give you money, they like to know a thing like that. He hesitates, thinking about going back, but decides against it.

He passes the graveyard and the church, and then the public house and the petrol pump. He walks again by the sludge of the canal, wondering if the greyhounds will come out, but they don't. A fast greyhound's worth a lot of money, the man with elephantiasis told him, knowing about such matters as a frequenter of greyhound tracks in the days before his body became a burden to him.

A thing happens. You can't change that. He looked up when the crane man shouted and then the crane man swung the bucket down, gentle as anything, getting it to the ground. He meant to tell them that, too. He had it ready, but in the end it got forgotten that the crane man had been gentle.

*

There is a quietness after Albert has gone, still there when the first wisps of twilight come. The room Thaddeus has always known, in which he searched beneath the sofa cushions for a ring that did not exist, is different now. There is an echo in the room, and in the hall and on the stairs. 'Everything is lovely here.'

His childhood past seems nothing much: the cruelty of love has damaged but not destroyed. To that Mrs Iveson might add that in her merciless mind's eye she sees, this evening, neither a husband lost to kind confinement nor a daughter's funeral. Her compassion faltered: shame creeps through guilt and feels like retribution.

The cups and saucers are gathered, the tea things stacked on Maidment's tray. Georgina's day is ending; she, too, is taken from the room. In time her curiosity will bring a mother back and offer misty images, like strangers vaguely present in a dream, of Eva Paczkowska and the husband who adored her. Again there will be dancing on the lawns, the hall door thrown open wide, music and voices on the cool night air. The laughter of Georgina's friends is waiting for Georgina's growing up, as the picture on the floor was waiting for her birth. The pets' memorials are waiting too, the summer-house built to catch the autumn sun, the gardener who showed his bayonet wound, servants remembered in a journal kept.

The coats hang on the hallstand pegs. In her party dress the child comes smiling down the stairs. Her Sunday uncle looks up from a leaflet he has finished reading. He smiles in turn, and reaches out for her. Afterwards there's Sunday tea.

Will there be offices built in the place? Thaddeus wonders. A supermarket? Will bright computer screens smudge away the nourishment of fantasy and delusion? Will check-out chatter silence the fearful whispering in grubby hide-aways, the soft enticements? Has defilement left no trace?

Will no one know among the tins of soup and processed peas that death was a balm here when it came? There was a life that ended for his onetime mistress, in its heyday a jolly, bouncing life. And for his wife there was a childhood softened by affection, and contentment later on, her goodness an enriching. The walls of a house were smashed to fragments, a bundle in the rubble lifted away: no life there'd been.

As the warmth of blood might miraculously seep into a shadow, or anaesthesia be lifted by a jolt, feelings he has never before experienced invade Thaddeus's solitude. The emotion stirred by the birth of his child was particular to that one event. His sadness was stony when he stood at the funeral of the wife he could not love. The flowers that Mrs Ferry so often longed for were sent when it was safe to send her flowers. Tonight he pities, and is angry.

The dusk is darkening when Mrs Iveson walks with Thaddeus in the garden, her stoic's stamina defeated in the pain of that same pity. A light comes on in a window of the house, then in another, a curtain's pulled across. High in the oak trees the rooks have settled on their branches. Below, among the shrubs and faded flowers, the single sound is Rosie's rustling in the sodden undergrowth, sniffing the fresh scent of moisture. The two do not walk close yet cling together, at one in honouring the ghost that has come to haunt this garden and this house.

★

'Albert.'

It is a whisper from what seems to be an empty doorway. He peers, and then a figure emerges, shaking off the dark, and it is Bev.

212

He speaks her name. He says he has been looking for her.

'I been around.'

'You OK, Bev?'

'I done with all that stuff. You know.'

'I wondered about you, Bev.'

'Yeah.' There is a silence, then Bev says: 'I ain't got nowhere to go nights.'

'You got work daytime?'

Bev shakes her head. She says she has tried for work, day work, nights, anything.

'You'd go for the Marmite factory? You'd go for anything like that?'

Bev says she would. The Marmite, the stocking place, up Chadwell, it doesn't matter.

'A woman told me they'll maybe be taking on at the stocking place.' Albert nods, lending emphasis to that. It would have been Tuesday he asked the woman, he remembers; it could be tomorrow they'll be taking on. 'Never does no harm to ask.'

They walk together, by the common, past the dairy yard. She isn't a tearaway, you wouldn't ever call Bev a tearaway and once she is taken on regular no way there'll be a problem with the rent. That's how he'll put it. There'll be reluctance at first, stands to reason there would be, but the rent will be the draw.

They cross Caspar Road. In the artificial light the blank shopfronts of Bride Street are tinged with orange. The KP Minimarket and Ishi Baba's take-away are secure behind their night grilles. Outside the Soft Rock Café the cat that is Albert's only enemy is rifling a dustbin.

'Turn of luck running into you, Bev.'

She says it was. She's tired. Albert can tell. She's dragging her footsteps a bit, the sole of a shoe flapping. Except to say it isn't far to Appian Terrace, he doesn't bother her with talk.

READ MORE IN PENGUIN

In every corner of the world, on every subject under the sun, Penguin represents quality and variety – the very best in publishing today.

For complete information about books available from Penguin – including Puffins, Penguin Classics and Arkana – and how to order them, write to us at the appropriate address below. Please note that for copyright reasons the selection of books varies from country to country.

In the United Kingdom: Please write to *Dept. EP, Penguin Books Ltd, Bath Road, Harmondsworth, West Drayton, Middlesex UB7 0DA*

In the United States: Please write to *Consumer Sales, Penguin Putnam Inc., P.O. Box 12289 Dept. B, Newark, New Jersey 07101-5289.* VISA and MasterCard holders call 1-800-788-6262 to order Penguin titles

In Canada: Please write to *Penguin Books Canada Ltd, 10 Alcorn Avenue, Suite 300, Toronto, Ontario M4V 3B2*

In Australia: Please write to *Penguin Books Australia Ltd, P.O. Box 257, Ringwood, Victoria 3134*

In New Zealand: Please write to *Penguin Books (NZ) Ltd, Private Bag 102902, North Shore Mail Centre, Auckland 10*

In India: Please write to *Penguin Books India Pvt Ltd, 11 Community Centre, Panchsheel Park, New Delhi 110017*

In the Netherlands: Please write to *Penguin Books Netherlands bv, Postbus 3507, NL-1001 AH Amsterdam*

In Germany: Please write to *Penguin Books Deutschland GmbH, Metzlerstrasse 26, 60594 Frankfurt am Main*

In Spain: Please write to *Penguin Books S. A., Bravo Murillo 19, 1° B, 28015 Madrid*

In Italy: Please write to *Penguin Italia s.r.l., Via Benedetto Croce 2, 20094 Corsico, Milano*

In France: Please write to *Penguin France, Le Carré Wilson, 62 rue Benjamin Baillaud, 31500 Toulouse*

In Japan: Please write to *Penguin Books Japan Ltd, Kaneko Building, 2-3-25 Koraku, Bunkyo-Ku, Tokyo 112*

In South Africa: Please write to *Penguin Books South Africa (Pty) Ltd, Private Bag X14, Parkview, 2122 Johannesburg*

BY THE SAME AUTHOR

Felicia's Journey
Winner of the 1994 Whitbread Book of the Year Award and the
Sunday Express Book of the Year Award

'A book so brilliant that it compels you to stay up all night galloping
through to the end . . . exquisitely crafted' *Daily Mail*. 'Immensely
readable . . . The plot twist – a characteristic mix – is both sinister and
affecting, and so skilfully done that you remember why authors have
plot twists in the first place' *Guardian*

Miss Gomez and the Brethren

Only the pub and the pet-shop are still inhabited in the boarded-up
wasteland of Crow Street in South-West London. Miss Gomez lives
for her postal correspondence with the Church of the Brethren of the
Way in Jamaica. No one will believe her revelation of a hideous sex
crime soon to be committed in Crow Street, until Prudence Tuke
disappears and the newspapers herald a 'Sex Crime Prophecy'. 'A
tender and passionate book as well as a very funny one' *Sunday Times*

His latest collection of short stories:

After Rain

'Each of the twelve stories in William Trevor's glittering collection,
After Rain, surveys a quietly devastating little earthquake. Tremors
that ensue when pressure is put on a fault-line running through a
marriage, family or friendship are traced with fine precision' *Sunday
Times*

Also published:

Two Lives	**Fools of Fortune**
The Old Boys	**The Boarding-House**
The Love Department	**The Silence in the Garden**
The Children of Dynmouth	**Ireland: Selected Stories**
Elizabeth Alone	**Outside Ireland: Selected Stories**
Mrs Eckdorf in O'Neill's Hotel	**The Collected Stories**
Other People's Worlds	